DIRTY CROWN

AMELIA WINTERS

Sign up for my newsletter to keep in touch. Find out about beta or ARC opportunities, get sneak peeks at new books, and have access to giveaways!

http://eepurl.com/hBcvpr

Want an exclusive extra scene of Everly and the Kings on Graduation day and the after party? Sign up and get it now!

COVINGTON HIGH SERIES

- Dirty Kingdom, book 1
- Dirty King, book 2
- Dirty Queen, book 3
- Dirty Court, book 4
- Dirty Reign, book 5
- Dirty Royals, book 6

- Dirty Crown, book 7
- Covington Christmas

THE SAVAGE DARK

- Lords of Darkness
- Dark Duplicity
- Deviant Darkness

CONTENTS

CHAPTER 1

I LAY ON THE CONCRETE FLOOR OF THE EMPTY OFFICE BUILDING several storeys below my Kings. They must think I lost my mind. If they even cared about my mind, that was.

After what they'd seen, I wouldn't blame them for never wanting to see me again.

I'd gotten my legs under me and made it a few levels lower, but had pushed the door into an empty, unfinished floor like the one we'd used for Maksim's holding. I hadn't made it far, though, because I'd fallen against a massive pillar and slid down to where I was now. I was staring out at the darkness beyond the floor to ceiling windows with my face pressed against the cold, rough floor.

I wasn't crying now, that was an improvement. I despised crying, the way my head filled up with pressure and the way my tears left streams and streaks across my skin. Mostly I hated how stuffed up I was, how I couldn't catch my breath or draw one in through my nostrils.

I was calm now. Well, not really calm but more like numb. I had locked all those feelings away again and I was able to be still and unfeeling even though the horror of what had just happened still enveloped my senses like inky black suffocating self-loathing.

It was the sheer terror I felt that had crippled me and left my emotions broken and non reactive. The terror that my Kings would find me just to express their absolute disgust at the things I'd done. That they would feel betrayed by my actions and they would hate me for them.

I couldn't face them.

I knew I'd been a coward before, especially when Maksim had broken me down, but now I was a fool on top of it. I should have gone to them first and confessed everything. I should have told them what I'd done and let them make their judgement in private, away from Avery and Maksim. If they had chosen to break it off, then I could have retained some of my dignity and gone back to handle this whole Ivan and Amara recovery on my own.

Now, if they dumped me, then it would be in front of everyone. I would be exposed, flayed and vulnerable with no way to deny what had happened.

Avery would mock me.

Maksim would come after me and there was be no reason for me not to go through with the wedding. I would be forced into a life of misery, all because I hadn't fought harder when he forced himself on me, and forced Avery to do those things to me.

I could still feel the way the gun felt pressed into my skin. My temple, under my jaw and into my neck, and my...

I couldn't even think about the other place he'd shoved the gone or I would dissolve into a mess of tears and snot again. My life was falling apart around me and I didn't know where to start to fix it. It felt like one thread had been pulled and now everything was unraveling. I couldn't escape the emotions I'd hidden for so long, and I couldn't pretend everything was okay when things hadn't been okay in the past. Trauma was a heavy burden to carry, and the longer you left it on your shoulders, the heavier it got until you stumbled once and the weight of it crushed you to the ground.

I sighed and a groan unintentionally left my mouth. My lungs were full of air, and I let the rest out so I could make it louder.

It echoed in the large space and I pushed myself off the floor. The cold had leeched into my flesh and was threatening to hit my bones if I didn't change my position.

"Fuck," I said and enjoyed the clapping echo of the word. "Fuck!" I repeated it louder, letting it dance all around me on sound waves.

I finally stood slowly, stretched my legs and walked to the window.

I was lower now, halfway down the building, and just barely over the lights of the city. They were still beautiful and still spread out ahead of me. If I hadn't just had my heard shattered, I could let myself enjoy this moment. The peace of it, the solitude as I sorted through my possible life choices. They were laid out before me like the lights of the city, close but not so distant that I couldn't touch them if I wanted.

I looked down at the street and saw headlights as a few cars wound through the maze like roads and I thought about what I had to do.

I had to prepare myself for the inevitable. The moment I saw it on the Kings' faces. The desire to leave me, to push me away and never see my disgusting, unfaithful, incestuous self again.

I took another deep breath and pressed the palms of my hands onto the window. I enjoyed the cool glass for a moment before turning and heading toward the stairwell once more.

I opened the door and half expected to hear them calling

for me, but there was nothing. Disappointment raced through me like shock and I knew they hated me then. I knew they wanted nothing to do with me.

So I wouldn't face the facts just yet. I couldn't.

I would sneak down to the street level and find myself somewhere to go. Somewhere far from the pressures of being hated by the men I loved. Far from the expectation of keeping my father and Amara alive and rescuing them. Far from giving everything up just to juggle the pressures of family, boyfriends, and my future.

I took my phone out and turned it off. I popped open the side of it, pulled out the SIM card and threw it on the floor. I cursed it under my heel and slipped the phone back into my pocket. Once I was a few blocks away, I would look for a throw away, something nobody could trace me with. Something I could call my own.

I felt relieved and insane. I couldn't tell if I was relieved or having a breakdown.

And I no longer cared.

* * *

ONE PART OF MY BIG PLAN THAT I HADN'T THOUGH THROUGH was the simple fact that I spoke no Czech. Not a single fucking word of it. I wasn't in a tourist area, either, where they would cater to North Americans and all speak English. I had to be in the kind of place only locals would know about or visit, either for work or entertainment.

There were a lot of small pubs and cafes as I got closer to the heart of the city, but none of them looked friendly to somebody like me.

It started to rain and the lights reflecting off the bright pavement were like a living watercolour painting. I felt like I was stepping into another world.

"Hey, fucking watch it," a man snarled as I bumped into him accidentally.

"Sorry," I replied and stepped wide to let him move past me on the sidewalk. As he kept going down the street, I thought of something. "Hey!" I called out.

He turned around, irritated. He was an older man wearing a wrinkled business suit and he was clutching a street map.

"What?" he barked in heavily accented English.

"How did you know I spoke English?" I asked.

"You're obviously American," he said with a dismissive wave of his hand. "You can always just tell."

"I'm having a bad day," I replied. "I don't usually look so crazy."

"It's not crazy, it's the way you carry yourselves," he said with smile. He shook his head and continued. "I'm sorry about your day, I hope it gets better."

He kept walking away, and even though he was probably more than double my age and was dressed in such a shabby way, he'd shown me the smallest amount of kindness. I wanted to follow him. Call it daddy issues or simply needing a hand in the middle of my mental storm, but he offered a stability that I needed.

"Hey, wait up," I said and jogged behind him until I caught up with his pace. "Where are you going?"

"To drink my cares away, if you must know," he said, bristling at my intrusion. "This is another American trait. You all think you belong everywhere."

"Where is there to drink around here?" I asked. I ignored his annoyance, maybe I was being relentlessly American, I didn't care. I need a human connection and my brain had chosen him.

"There's a small bar up there," he said. "It's not a bad place, one of the cleaner in this area."

"Are you going there?" I asked.

"Yes," he relied and kept walking. Then he took a deep breath and sighed so long I didn't know if he remembered how to breathe. "I know I'm going to regret this, but do you want to join me?"

"Yes!" I said, a little too eager. "I need something to calm my nerves."

I trotted with him as he sped up. He was my height but he was fast for an old guy.

We went a couple blocks and he turned into a darkened building that didn't look like anything great from the outside. The inside was okay, and it was clearly somewhere to drink.

That's all I wanted, something to ease my nerves.

He sat at the bar and I sat next to him. He cleared his throat and motioned for the bartender.

There were maybe fifteen or twenty tables and booths scattered around the dimly lit place and almost all of them were occupied by one or two people quietly sipping their drinks.

The man ordered his, a scotch, and I ordered a gin and tonic. I wasn't even legal to drink in the US, but here it didn't seem to matter. When my companion translated my order for me, the bar tender didn't even break stride.

Once we got our drinks, the man beside me said, "Well, are you going to tell me why it's a bad day?"

"It's almost impossible to describe," I said. "If I told you everything, you'd never believe me."

"Try me," he grunted and sipped his scotch. "I've seen some things, believe."

"I was kidnapped," I said and then shook my head. "No, this goes back farther. My father left me when I was a baby and my mom had to raise me on her own..."

With that, I launched into my life's story, which was

arguably one of the craziest things the man had ever heard even if he pretends like it wasn't.

I didn't tell him everything, I couldn't. I didn't tell him what kind of abuse Reg had committed on me, for one. I just let him think I shot Reg because of self defence.

And I didn't tell him about The Organization. I mean, how could I?

And I didn't tell him how I'd just been assaulted by Maksim and Avery, or any of the family shit. In fact, he was shocked by my story and I glossed over at least fifty percent of it.

But it helped. As I was laying it out in the open for him, I realized that I wasn't weak or feeble. I realized that I deserved to have more credit than I gave myself. I had survived so much insanity it was amazing that I wasn't mentally destroyed by now.

But I knew why that was. Without the support of four men, my four pillars of strength, I would have lost myself long ago.

So there in the dark little tavern with a complete stranger, I decided that no matter how my Kings felt about me, I was going to fight to keep them in my life.

And after about five drinks, I even told the man about them. He was shocked but not that shocked. He seemed almost impressed even and expressed the fact that he wanted to meet them.

"I might have gotten back on the relationship horse if I had four hot men waiting for me," he'd chuckled and taken a sip.

He was in the middle of telling me about his own history with love and loss, when he got his wish.

"So there I was, dumped and broken hearted and age forty three, dumped by the nicest guy I'd ever dated," he told me, leaning in close. I was drunk enough that I'd forgotten about everything and was hanging on his story. "When I decided to turn my back on love, I'd already gone through several break ups and a few long term relationships. I was done. But you know what?"

"What?" I asked, mesmerized by his wisdom.

"I didn't—"

His sentence was cut short as he was lifted out of his seat by the collar of his cheap suit. It took me a second to realize what was going on, and then I looked up into Ryker's blazing eyes as he held the man above the floor.

"What the fuck are you doing to her?" Ryker roared and Kingston gathered close and glaring down at the man.

"Get the fuck away from her," Kingston growled and shot the man such a menacing look that I didn't think he harbored any more fantasies about having four of these beasts around. "What have you done? Why does she look like she's crying?"

"I was crying!" I exclaimed and grabbed at Ryker and Kingston. I was too tipsy to be that effective, but they got the point. Ryker released the man's collar, and Kingston stepped back. "I was crying because of what happened!"

"It wasn't him?" Kingston asked, glaring at the man. The man shrunk back but raised his eyebrows and gave me an approving look.

"No, it was the situation," I hissed. "It was what you saw."

"You mean about you and—"

"We'll talk about it in private," I warned them. I would die if they mentioned it in front of my newfound friend.

"Come back with us, princess," Ryker insisted. "You must come with us. We have business to conduct and things to talk about."

He kept giving the man side eye looks, as if he was worried the man would understand what he was talking about.

Kingston finally took my face in his hands to get my attention, got up really close and pinned me with an intense look in the eyes.

"Princess, if you don't get your ass back to the group, shit is going to hit the fan and everything will be lost."

It was the way he said it, like he was in complete command of every thought I had, every movement I made. I melted somewhere inside and gave myself completely to him. To him and the Kings.

"Looks like your men are calling you home," the man, my new friend, said and sipped his whiskey. "And if I were you, I'd listen."

He gave each of my Kings a long, lust filled look up and down and winked at me.

I grinned, nodded, and we said our goodbyes but not before he tapped out his contact information in my phone.

On the way out, once we hit the fresh, crisp night air, the alcohol buzz wore off me and I remembered why I had run away in the first place.

"Oh god," I said as the memory of them watching Maksim's video reared up inside my mind. "I'm going to be sick."

And I bent over on a sidewalk in Prague and threw up with a King on either side of me.

It occurred to me somewhere in the midst of my misery that they weren't going anywhere.

They were going to give me a chance.

CHAPTER 2

"Ilya got back to us and we have to meet him in person," Kingston explained as we walked back to the empty building. "It's urgent, and I don't know if I fully trust him so we need you there to negotiate."

"Why did you run away, princess?" Ryker asked, putting his arm around my shoulder. "What made you so upset?"

I almost couldn't say it. It was so dreadful it felt like if I let it out into the world it would grow legs and take on a life of its own.

But they'd come for me, and from what I could tell, Archer and Valen were just as concerned but they'd stayed back to watch Maksim and Avery.

"It was the video," I said, and an involuntary shudder raced through my body. Ryker's arm squeezed me tighter and he kissed the top of my head. Kingston took my hand in his and held me close.

"The video was horrible, I'm not gonna lie," Kingston said at last. "I almost couldn't watch it. In fact I had to look away after a couple seconds of it."

"Because I was cheating on you four," I wailed, and tears

threatened to spill. "I was doing horrible things with my own sister. I'm a disgusting human being, how could you love me?"

Ryker tensed up and Kingston dropped my hand immediately, confirming my worst fears. I bunched up my muscles, preparing to run again, when the craziest thing happened.

Ryker spun me to face him, pulled me close to his chest and wrapped his arms around me. Kingston stood behind me and squished me between their two massive, muscled bodies, filling me with warmth, security and love.

"Why are you sandwiching me?" I asked, my lip threatening to quiver with emotion.

"What I saw was the woman I love being assaulted by a fucking pig," Ryker said through gritted teeth. "I saw you enduring humiliation because you had no other choice."

"I saw you keeping yourself alive when a fucking deviant madman tried to destroy you," Kingston said, the bass from his voice rumbling against my back. "You survived for us, babe. You suffered for us. So you could make it back to us and let us help you."

"You did whatever you had to in order to survive," Ryker agreed and kissed the top of my head again. "That's all I saw, you making your way home to us."

Their love broke me, but in a good way this time. It didn't destroy me, like Maksim had done. It broke down the walls I'd been building around my heart since I'd gotten away from Ilya and his sociopathic son.

They didn't tear them down completely, but they broke through enough that brightness shone through, the light from their love for me incinerated the shadow thoughts that had been growing in the dank darkness.

I wanted to tell them this, but all that squeaked past my lips was a small sigh of disbelief. I'd spent so many years hating myself, filled with self loathing, that I didn't believe it when they loved me. I didn't believe them, that they could want a woman such as myself.

If only they knew how horrible I was on the inside, how terrible my thoughts sometimes were, they would despise me more than I did myself.

"Come on, princess," Ryker said, breaking my silent shock. He brushed a tear off my cheek with the back of his hand and kissed me on the forehead. "We need to get back and then we're going to show you how much we love you."

"We'll spend a lifetime proving it to you," Kingston said and put his arm around me as we started to walk. We switched positions and I took Ryker's hand.

In all my tipsiness, I had forgotten where I was and would have been completely lost without them.

I felt sick to my stomach when I thought about how weak I was and how easy it was for me to fall apart when I experienced something stressful and on my own. I needed my Kings, that much was certain, otherwise I was a complete emotional disaster.

We walked slowly, carefully, with me leaning on Ryker and then Kingston and back again. I couldn't help but worry about what they truly thought, though, because as much as I loved being with them, the chaos inside wouldn't let me rest.

I still couldn't believe that such incredible men could love somebody like me.

That was the crux of it all, I had such crippling self loathing that I couldn't fathom myself having any value.

At least that's what it felt like now, in the light of day when my spine was straight and I was kicking ass, I could silence the whispers from time to time.

Once we got to the building, everything began to feel like it was making sense again. I felt as if all the millions of cuts that had torn me apart earlier in the night were covering over. They were healing and patching themselves up.

With each step I felt like I was getting stronger and clearer headed. We rode the elevator up to the penthouse, and the moment I stepped out, I was surrounded by all four of them again.

Valen and Archer were almost inconsolable in their panic. I felt horrible that I'd done it to them, so I pulled them both against me and let them just hold me for a couple of moments before stepping back.

"I can't believe I ever doubted how you would feel," I said as my alcohol high wore off. "What happened to me back there?"

"You've gone through a lot, babe," Valen said, rubbing my shoulder. "Fuck, anybody's mind would crack if they went through half of what you've endured."

"I'm sorry I didn't notice how much you were suffering," Archer said and hung his head. "I feel ashamed that I didn't see your pain. I was so fucking caught up in all of this that I didn't see how it hurt you."

"That, too," Ryker agreed. "I feel like a piece of shit about it. I hid my own injuries from y'all, I should have picked up that you were doing the same."

"I think we all need the time to do an inventory of hurts and injuries, both emotional and physical," Kingston said. "But not now, after we figure this shit out, okay?"

And then he turned to me and took my face in his huge, strong hands, looked me in the eye and added, "Promise you won't run away again. Promise me you'll let us know when you're falling apart. We can't fix it if we don't know it's broken, and the thought of you breaking when you're in front of us absolutely fucking guts me, princess. So promise me you'll trust us with your care and support when you desperately need it, okay?"

Tears prickled my eyes and I nodded my agreement, unable to speak.

Everything felt like it had clicked back into place. Like the gears of the universe aligned again and the world was turning on its axis the way it should have been all along. It was my head that had thrown it off its balance, and my own fearful, furtive imaginings that had almost destroyed everything.

I was broken inside, I could see that now. But I was also healing. Eventually these breakdowns would become fewer and farther between as I knitted myself back together with help from my Kings.

"Okay," I said at last, not exactly wanting to give up the sensation of their hands on me, comforting and supporting me. But...we had business to get to. "We need to move these two. Wait, has Avery been loose this entire time?"

I looked around in shock, half expecting to see her crouched in the corner with a cell phone or gone from the building all together and on her way to call Ilya.

"No, we tied her up," Valen said with a lopsided grin. "I can't stand her, and she wouldn't stop talking. She hits on us constantly and honestly? I wish I could have shut her up back at Fincross but I know it's not acceptable out in the real world."

"But here? Fuck yeah, I'll run a strip of duct tape across her mouth in a heartbeat," Archer chuckled. "Seriously, when you're not around it's nonstop from her. And she doesn't get it, she doesn't understand how we're so focused on you, and you alone, princess."

We walked across the open space and just around the large concrete pillar in the middle of the room, I found Avery bound and gagged and glared up at me with pure hatred.

She was on her side, her wrists and ankles were taped up, and her mouth was covered. She looked miserable, and I didn't exactly revel in it, I did appreciate the fact that my

Kings didn't want to hear her spew her bullshit so they shut her down.

"She's never had anybody loyal to her," I said, looking down with pity. I knew the pity would hurt her more than anger. I nudged her with the toe of my boot and continued. "She sees Maksim and how he'll fuck anybody that slows down long enough to let him slip his little dick inside. She can't believe that all men aren't like that, low down slippery and unfaithful."

"Sad," Kingston said, looking down next to me. "Anyhow, she's not the one we're worried about. We need to get this piece of shit on the move before they figure out where they are."

"But first," Ryker said, stepping forward to the chair where Maksim was still bound and gagged. "We want to help you get a little revenge."

"What do you mean?" I asked.

"I want to put a bullet in his head, but we need him," Kingston growled, stepping towards him with such a long stride that the confident defiance fled from Maksim's face and he blanched white in fear.

"So we decided you get to do what you want," Archer said. "From the neck down, and he has to be alive at the end of it."

"Well that rules out what I really want," I said, pondering the terrible things I could do to him.

"That's what I said," Valen said from beside me. "But then again, that's what we all want. Even Avery, I'm sure, if we asked her."

Maksim glanced down at the floor along with the rest of us. Down there, Avery shook her head and pleaded to him with her eyes. She wouldn't want him to know how she disliked him, her life depended on Maksim thinking she worshipped the ground he walked on.

"So anything?" I asked, scanning his body for the things I

could do. "I'd like to cut his dick off, but that wouldn't make much difference."

My Kings laughed and Maksim winced, but glared. He shot me daggers and I would be dead if he could kill from a distance.

"What about his balls?" Ryker asked, producing a large hunting knife. I had no idea where he'd been keeping it on his body, but Ryker was a man of constant surprises. I had a feeling he wasn't planning on getting caught without being prepared ever again.

"He'll bleed out," I said. "At least that's what I've heard."

"He will," Kingston said, not taking his eyes off Maksim. "There's much to green t a risk and we need this piece of shit alive. For now."

"I have an idea," I said, thinking of the fear I'd felt when Maksim had pressed the gun to my head and the absolute soul shattering horror of him fucking me with the muzzle. I reached for Ryker's knife and he handed it to me, carefully holding the blade while presenting me the handle.

"You're so fucking beautiful when you're violent," Kingston said as he exhaled an awe filled breath.

"Absolutely fucking stunning," Archer agreed.

He stepped behind me and kissed the back of my neck and I shivered in anticipation and from the sensation of his mouth on my flesh.

Valen ran his hand down my back and slid his hand down my pants until his hand was touching skin to skin on my ass, cupping it. The feeling was powerful, and with each touch, my Kings drove the helplessness and fear I'd been carrying out of my body. They knew what I needed to feel their support, and they knew how much I had to have them beside me, touching me, inside of me.

As I sized up Maksim, I looked back down at Avery. She wasn't innocent in all of this, but she was a victim in her own right. I didn't want to eek out revenge on her, but I also didn't want to worry about her coming after me for what I was about to do.

I dropped to my knees and held the knife to her neck. I pressed it into the skin until a line of beaded blood appeared and she gasped in pain. Tears formed in her eyes and I smiled at her.

"I'm going to lose my shit here in a minute," I told her, not breaking eye contact. "I'm gonna go off the fucking rails. So understand that this is for your own good, you got that?"

She was confused, and I didn't blame her, but she needed her head anyhow.

My Kings waited, watching as I drew my hand back and gripped the knife handle.

They had no idea if I was going to slit her neck or stab her in the chest, but they were going to support me no matter what and I loved them deeply for that.

I didn't hurt Avery, though, I simply took the butt end of the knife and slammed it down into her temple.

The blow was swift and hard and knocked her out immediately. Once I was sure she wasn't going to see what I was going to do, I turned to my Kings and said, "I need you to do something for me, and it might seem weird."

"Anything you want," Ryker said, and I glanced down. He was hard already.

And I knew they weren't going to say no.

CHAPTER 3

I took Valen's hand and put it back on my ass, then pulled Ryker closer for a kiss to reward him for having the knife.

I reached for Kingston and drew him to me, and did the same for Archer. I could feel their hard cocks pressing into me on either side.

"I need this," I told them. "I don't know why, but I fucking need this so bad right now."

"I know why, and I know what you need," Ryker said, shoving his hand down the front of my pants, pushing them over my hips and leaving me bare. I was covered by my Kings, so Maksim couldn't see what was happening but I was certain he understood. Ryker's hand cupped my mound and his finger split my cleft, finding my clit and immediately going to work.

Kingston pulled my face to his and kissed me deeply as Valen sought my slick heat from behind.

Archer went under my shirt and rolled my nipple between his fingers while kissing my exposed neck. I clutched the knife handle in my hand and let myself rock on waves between the four of them. They passed me around, not physically, but intuitively they each applied pressure and pleasure at different times so it was like sound waves racing around a cyclonic space, around and around as the energy transferred.

I gasped as it reached a fevered pitch, and I pushed forwards to the chair where Maksim sat, frozen in fascination and fear.

"I can't see his face and still want to feel this good," I said, and motioned for Kington's jacket. He took it off and I tossed it over Maksim's head, so he couldn't get any pleasure out of this. He was such a sick fucking bastard that part of him would enjoy what I was about to do as long as there was sex involved.

"What's your poison, princess?" Ryker asked, slipping his finger across my clit then sliding it forward to push inside of me. He had to crouch in order to do this, and I inhaled the scent of him while he was down so close. His hair and skin smelled so good, musky and woodsy even though I didn't think he'd chopped a tree in his life.

"I'm going to make him hurt," I gasped as they worked my body again, this time in front of Maksim's chair. "I want him to remember me and how he has no power over me."

"I'll fucking remember you, you bitch," Maksim said, shaking his head to try and dislodge the jacket. "I'll remember the look on your face when I'm gutting you like a fish. I'm going to slit a hole in your stomach and fuck it like a bloody little cunt!"

Kingston couldn't help himself, he backhanded Maksim as hard as he could, making the chair spin away and hit the pillar behind it. Maksim let out a grunt of pain at the same moment Ryker hit my clit again, and I groaned in pleasure.

"I have to do this," I rasped and we edged forward like

some bizarre, multi limbed creature. "I want to make him pay."

"I wish we could kill him," Archer said. "Fuck, I wish we could."

"I'd cut his throat for you," Valen told me, his hand deep in my pants. God, I loved them all, so willing to leap on board my crazy train and able to keep up with my wild mood swings. One minute I was running from them all because I worried they'd think I was unfaithful, the next I was getting them to get me off while I was carving up my enemy.

I guess if anything could be said about me, it was that I was a wild fuck.

They continued to pleasure me while I lifted my hand, grabbed Maksim's shirt with the other, and tore it open, exposing his chest.

"What are you doing, you sick cunt?" he said from under the jacket. I could hear him choking on something, Kingston's hit might have made him bleed and the image of that drove me harder.

"I'm doing something to think about the next time you want to hurt a woman," I hissed and spread the shirt wide.

Ryker's fingers played with my clit, Valen's fucked my pussy from behind, Kingston and Archer played with my breasts and kissed my neck, and I lifted the knife for my release. The icing on the cake, the cherry on top. The sweet sensation of revenge as I hit my orgasm.

Just as I got there, I slid the knife against Maksim's left nipple, areola and all. He screamed and twisted to get away as I cut it clean off. I tossed it to the side, and he kicked and pushed so hard that Kingston had to leave my breast and hold him steady.

"I've got this, princess," he said and looked at me with fire and admiration in his eyes. "I've got you, Evie."

Maksim screamed, unintelligible noises of agony, but I wasn't over yet.

Ryker and Valen worked my pussy, Archer worked my breasts, and I sliced off Maksim's other nipple. This one was a larger area of skin and it began to bleed immediately, catching up to the other.

I stood back, Kingston let him go and held me upright as I came in his arms. I clung to him while the other Kings brought me wave after wave of release, until I was breathless and unable to handle any more.

They knew, they always did. They played my body like it was an instrument, and they always knew when to let me gather myself back together.

The four of them surrounded me and I let the knife drop to the concrete floor with a clatter. I began to sob, from relief of being in their arms again and from joy at my revenge. They didn't hate me, in fact they loved me enough to help me in my wild desires.

The sounds of Maksim's groans and sobs lifted me even higher, and I knew I should have never run from these men. They were my ride or die posse, extensions of my own life, and the reason for me to carry on.

I couldn't imagine being anywhere else, and I couldn't imagine being with anybody but them.

My Kings, my saviors, and my loves.

My life.

* * *

"Get his shirt back together and put Kingston's jacket on him or they'll see the blood," I said, motioning toward Maksim's prone body. We'd cut him out of the chair and he was lying on the floor next to Avery and they were both out cold. We'd given Maksim some sedative because he wouldn't stop whining and crying about the pain, and Avery was still out. I guess I'd hit her pretty hard, and although I hoped she woke up, I wasn't exactly going to be broken up about it if she didn't. I was feeling savage about it all, and her death wouldn't faze me in that moment.

"Good call," Valen said, lifting Maksim so Archer could help him with the jacket. Maksim's white shirt was stained with twin blooming roses of blood on the front. His nipples were gone, and the blood was slowing, but it was still pretty obvious something had happened to him. When we got on the line with Ilya, I wanted Maksim to appear intact.

We were just getting ready to leave Prague. We'd found the pilot who brought us here. He was still in the city, and we were going to meet him in half an hour.

So far, we'd been lucky because there had been no sign of Ilya or his men, and Maksim hadn't been his usual annoying, demanding self now that I cut him down to size. He had, however, need to chill the fuck out for the drive over there, because the thought of being trapped in the SUV with him crying about his nipples, oh his nipples, they were erogenous zones, then I was going to scream.

"Got it," Archer said, and we propped him up between the two of them. They were going to get him down to street level, and Kingston would pull the SUV around while Ryker and I helped Avery down.

It somehow went off without a hitch. There were a couple moments when we dropped them, and once when Avery's hair got caught in the elevator doors when it closed at first. I had visions of her being scalped as we started going down, so I'd hit every button until the doors and opened again and we could free her up.

The bitch owed me one. If she survived.

Before I knew it, we were off to the private airport to fly away on the unregistered private jet. The key was that it was unregistered, otherwise Ilya could track our flight and figure out where we were going.

As it was, we had decided on flying to London to hide out in a flat that Ivan kept there.

The more I got to know about Ivan, the more I realized he was one of those guys I ranted about back in college. The millionaire/billionaire class who bought up property in every big city and then left it sitting empty for most of the time.

My own father was a land hoarding dick, and I'd have to talk to him about it once we got him free. We could become the shady possibly criminal family that used their money for social benefits, not just greed and unnecessary consumption.

Until then, I'd take advantage of the private jet and access to money and have no guilt about it. I had to go easy on myself, I was still reeling from my overreaction to Maksim's video. And by overreaction, I don't mean the nipple slicing or the running away, I mean the fact that I ever doubted my Kings and their support through all of this.

It was insane to me now looking back on it, how I could have ever thought they'd turn their backs on me for something that was out of my control. I still felt dirty and shameful about it, and sort of like I cheated even though logically that made no sense, but I also felt loved by all of them. Every time they loved me, they left me better than I was before. Stronger, more determined, and healthier.

"You look pensive," Archer said, watching me from the seat across the aisle. "You're not regretting your decision, are you?"

"You mean my decision to leave Maksim's nipple back there on the floor?" I asked with a grin. "Yeah, I regret not bringing them with us so I could make a lovely set of earrings."

I held my fingers to my earlobes to pantomime dangling jewelry.

He winced and made a gagging face, but Ryker laughed loudly next to me.

"Now why didn't I think of that?" he exclaimed. "I'd wear a pair."

"That's expected," Kingston chuckled and closed his eyes again, pretending to sleep in the chair across from me. He didn't love flying and did best when he was dozing or doing dirty things with me. Since we had hostages, and the flight attendant was so close by, and it wasn't our private plane, there was nothing dirty being done at the moment.

I wouldn't have minded, however. I was still throbbing from the thrill of slicing into my captor's flesh while my Kings played my body like a finely tuned instrument. God, there was something wrong with me. Something deeply fucked.

But I didn't care. I only cared that I was okay now, I had my loves, and I could indulge my darker fantasies every now and again. Back home when we were boring again, and this whole thing was over, I could play with them and find out if I enjoyed receiving pain or just giving it. I could see the five of us experimenting with more bondage type scenarios, blood play even, nothing too painful of course.

Even now just thinking about it made me squirm in my seat. I was getting myself heated just from the image of my four Kings on their knees in front of me, worshipping my pussy and letting me do whatever I wanted with them.

I let my lids drop and my imagination travel, thinking of cutting them just enough for a single bead of blood to bloom on their skin so I could draw my tongue across it and—

"You're thinking about sex, aren't you?" Valen said, interrupting my fantasy.

I looked up at him and he was standing by my seat

leaning over and looking down. I blushed and fluttered my lashes.

"Uh, well," I stammered.

"I could tell," he said with a crooked smile. "You were licking your lips and had that look on your face."

"What look?" I asked, a little alarmed that I wasn't the sophisticated poker faced mysterious woman I thought I was.

"The look like you're about to dive into an all you can eat buffet," he laughed. "Like you're going to stuff yourself until you can't fit another thing into that tight, sexy body of yours."

"He's right," Archer said. "You always look at us like we're just big pieces of meat to you. I feel harassed."

"What?" I gulped. "I don't think that!"

"You don't?" Ryker asked and nudged me with his shoulder. "I'm disappointed you don't objectify me, princess. I work hard on this body so you'll treat me like your private fuck doll."

"Did somebody say fuck doll?" Kingston asked, opening his eyes. "I'll wake up for that, if that's what we're doing."

He smiled at me with an eager look, his fake sleep long gone the minute he thought sex might be on the table.

"Nobody's fucking any doll," I said, waving my hand in front of me. "In fact, nobody's fucking anybody right now."

"You've got that right," the flight attendant said, rushing down the aisle towards us. "Your, uh, passengers are waking up and they're pissed."

From behind the screened off area where we'd unceremoniously dumped Maksim and Avery, I heard a racket. Maksim bellowed about killing us all, and Avery was groaning and moaning about what a cunt I was.

I sighed, looked around at my Kings and shrugged my shoulders.

"I guess one of us has to deal with this.

"This is why we need more sex talk," Valen said as he stood up. "It makes shit like this easier to deal with."

And as I stood up to follow him and my other Kings, I had to say I agreed.

I needed a good fuck after all of this, but I didn't know when we'd ever get the time.

CHAPTER 4

Maksim yelled so much on the plane that we gave him another sedative and slapped a strip of tape across his mouth, just to be certain he'd shut the fuck up. He was so annoying when he was in pain and experiencing discomfort. The irony wasn't lost on me, since he was such a piece of shit to anybody he had captive and now here he was, the biggest wimp when it came to his trauma.

We landed in London in the early morning, just as the mist was rising on the tarmac of the airfield. We were outside of town, but there was another car and driver there to meet us and take us to the flat.

It wasn't some old style London brick and limestone townhouse, though, not like I was expecting. It was the penthouse in a sleek new glass building in a wealthy district. Ivan and his penthouses. I'd have to ask him about that sometime. It was as if he couldn't stand the thought of anybody on top of him, he had to be top dog at all times.

When we were inside the apartment and away from prying eyes at last, we propped Maksim up on a leather sofa with Avery on the other end. She was awake, but perhaps slightly out of it because she was much more mellow than usual. Or maybe my blow to her head had rattled something around and would make her a nicer human being. I'd have to consider it my charitable service, if that was the case.

"We should send another video to Ilya," Kingston said, and he ran his hand through his hair while taking a deep breath. He looked bone tired. We all did. We were weary of being on the run or from being hyped up on adrenaline for so many days now.

"We'll do a quick video, and then bed," I said. "I want to be in this one, though. I'm tired of hiding from him."

They all nodded, and we got set up straight away.

Kingston held the burner phone and recorded me next to Maksim. I sat up straight, crossed my legs, and placed my hands on my knee while the phone rang. He picked up and I could hear him breathing on the other end.

"Hello Ilya, I understand you've had time to go over our previous demands," I said and braced myself for his response.

"Fuck you!" he bellowed, breaking his silence. "Fuck you, you fucking cunt! Maksim! Come on, boy, fight back!"

He added a bunch in Russian, but I didn't understand the language. Given Ilya's way with words, it was probably more of the same as what he'd been saying.

"He's a little sleepy at the moment," I told the furious father. "But he's still eager to get home. Now, where is Ivan?"

The last video we sent demanded that Ivan be present for the next live chat.

Ilya muttered something in Russian to somebody off camera, and in moments Ivan was dragged into view.

They deposited my father at Ilya's feet. He tumbled forward and fell in a crumpled heap, barely having the strength to look up at the camera. His eyes sought mine, as if he could see me over the miles and miles and he could see into my soul.

I hadn't had a lifetime to get to know my father, and I hadn't grown up worshipping him as his little girl. I didn't even know if I loved him now, my heart was so closed off that only having him in my life for a couple years meant I needed time to warm up to him.

But despite all of that, seeing him like that was a knife to the guts. A sharp pain followed by a twisting sensation that ramped it up. It was if there was a tear in the fabric of the universe, a shifting in time or a wavering of reality.

Ivan, the entire time I'd known him, had been larger than life. Almost inhuman with his power and skills and the way he handled himself. He commanded attention everywhere he went, not just from his powerful physical presence, but also from his powerful energy.

The man before us now was half of who he'd been. Ilya had starved Ivan, that much was obvious. He was like a prisoner of war, with his skin stretched across his skeletal frame. His muscles had wasted away in the time Ivan had been captured. He looked like he was battling an illness not just battling to stay alive.

"Tell her you're okay," Ilya said with a smirk as he poked Ivan with the toe of his boot. "Tell her you're happy staying with me. It's been like a vacation. Or summer camp. Like one of those fun sleep over situations where we get to spend so much time together."

Ivan's eyes focused on the camera again, and he coughed before giving a wan smile. He was hurting, his pain apparent with each breath he took. He winced and tensed up, as if he had broken ribs, or had been beaten enough that it hurt to breathe.

"It's been a blast," he said with a grim tone and his lips pressed into a thin line. "Such a fucking blast. Don't worry about me, daughter dear, worry about yourself."

"Are you injured?" I asked. "How badly?"

Ivan scoffed and said, "Minimally. Ilya has been trying to crush me but he doesn't have the balls to do the job."

Ilya cursed him out in Russian and kicked him with his foot. I looked at him, narrowed my eyes and said, "What happens there, happens here."

With Ilya watching intently, leaning forward to see exactly what I was doing, I stood up and lifted my leg. I was wearing boots of my own, and deliberately drew my foot back and slammed it into Maksim's knee. Maksim grunted in his sleep and groaned.

"Do it again, and your son will suffer," I said, moving towards the camera so I would block Maksim out. "Keep doing it and neither one of us will have somebody to trade."

"You fucking bitch!" Ilya exclaimed, keeping up with his usual high level of language. "You hurt my son, you're fucking dead. Fucking dead, I tell you! Dead!"

"I look pretty alive right now," I said and shrugged. "Besides, if you come for me, I have four men who will be coming after you. And they're just rich enough to do it physically or financially. Either way, you and your empire are fucked if you mess with me."

Ilya leaned over and gestured to somebody off camera. A man in a security suit stepped forward and bent down to speak with him. Ilya gestured and talked into the man's ear, and the man nodded in agreement as Ilya gave his instruction. The man replied and then stood up, Ilya looked back at the camera and said, "Okay, we can make a deal."

"The only deal I'm interested in is getting Ivan and Amara back alive," I said. "I want both of them for your son, and I'll even throw in Avery for shits and giggles."

He frowned and said, "You didn't mention a damned thing about Amara, I don't even know if we still have her."

"Then you'd better find her," I replied and I sat down next to Maksim once more. I grabbed a handful of his hair and lifted his head up. He groaned and tried to pull away from me, even in his sleep. His fear fed my boldness and his pain emboldened my plans. "Because if you don't, you can kiss this pretty boy goodbye."

I kissed Maksim on the cheek and he visibly reacted by trying harder to get away. Even Ilya must have noticed how scared his precious son was, because his face fell and a flicker of emotion crossed it.

As fast as it appeared, it was gone again. He scowled and said, "Contact me within twelve hours and we'll know where she is. Until then, don't you dare hurt him. Don't you fucking dare."

"I'll treat him with all the respect and kindness you've shown my father," I said and flashed an evil grin just before I dragged my finger across my neck, both a gesture of threat to Ilya and motioning for the session to be over. Kingston understood, cut off the recording, and slipped the phone into his pocket.

"I think that went well," I laughed, but the tension in my voice made it sound brittle. "Well, it went okay. At least he's still alive. They'd better fucking pray Amara is found, and that she's okay or I'll cut Maksim's throat before he has a chance to call for his daddy."

"For Maksim's sake, I hope they find her," Kingston said and pulled me into his arms. I didn't mind leaving Maksim on the couch to be embraced, I needed the comfort. The other three Kings surrounded me and I got my group huddle, all the love and support I craved just then.

"I need sleep," I said. "Can we tie them up again and get some rest?"

"Yes, please," Ryker said, and we made quick work of it. Avery was more awake than she'd been before, and she fought against me binding her hands and feet with zip ties and duct tape. I left her mouth free, so she could breathe. But if she started to scream, I promised her I'd slap it on her face in a heartbeat.

Maksim woke up as we were doing his, but he was subdued more than normal. I took this as a good sign, that maybe he was learning his place among us. I preferred to see him mentally beaten down. I liked knowing that I had bested him, that my violence had finally been the thing to shut him up.

He'd pushed me first, and he hadn't expected me to bite back. I supposed it wasn't his fault. I definitely crumbled during the whole ordeal, but he didn't understand how I always came back swinging. I always made it through my break downs and came out the other side stronger and better for it.

I wasn't going to let him see me like that ever again. I wouldn't show him my vulnerability, he would see nothing but my strength.

So it was good that he kept to himself and kept his eyes downcast as we bound him tight.

"You'd better get some sleep," I told him after we'd finished and pushed him onto his side on the sofa. "Tomorrow is going to be a very long day, and you're going to need every ounce you can get."

He sighed and nodded, then closed his eyes. It felt strange, because I was almost sorry for him. With a father like Ilya, there hadn't been much of a chance for him to be a decent human being.

Still, I could feel sorry for him and not let myself get suckered into his evil games.

And besides, I had a bed with four guys waiting for me. Maksim would be just find on his own, out here with Avery for comfort and warmth.

The two of them deserved each other.

* * *

"WHAT ARE WE DOING FOR BREAKFAST?" ARCHER ASKED AS HE rolled over to where I was curled under the blankets and pretending I wasn't awake. "Valen and Ryker offered to cook, but I don't mind going out for something if that's what you want."

I opened one eye, peered out, and said, "How did you know I was awake?"

"Oh, come on, princess," he chuckled. "There's not much you can keep from us, you know. You breathe differently, for one. And I don't know, I could just sense it."

"Your spidey senses tingled?" I asked with a smile.

"My something tingled, that's for sure," he laughed. "But I'm hungrier than I am horny and I assume you're the same."

"I think we're all the same," I replied. "Is there anything to eat in here?"

"It's been stocked. It's almost as if somebody knew we were coming," he replied.

"Most likely it's Ivan's wasteful planning," I grumbled, even though it was saving my ass right now. "He keeps his main apartments fully stocked and staffed just in case he wants to drop in at any time."

"I'm sure somebody gets the food before it goes bad, my little environmentalist," Archer said and pulled back the covers without warning. He dove on me and nuzzled my neck while I squirmed and screamed. "I know you care, but sometimes it's not the end of the world if he doesn't recycle everything."

I laughed and gasped and had to agree. I didn't understand why I was so peeved at Ivan's plan other than the fact that I was putting my stress onto something that felt like I could control. Everything else with Ivan was so beyond my control at the moment, it felt good to complain about his lack of recycling.

Breakfast was simple, just eggs and toast with a side of pancakes. Archer loved making the pancakes, but I secretly thought he just liked the showmanship of the event. He basked in everybody's attention as he dramatically flipped them over the frying pan.

After breakfast, we had to decide if we should feed Avery and Maksim, if they deserved it.

"They did leave me trapped without food for a couple of days," I said, remembering the pinch of hunger.

"Then they should starve." Valen picked up his plate and wafted his hand across it, as if to send the delicious scent of food towards the two prisoners in the other room.

"As much as I'd love to see them squirm," I replied, eyeing them up from the kitchen. They were uncomfortable and letting it be known through constant shifting and dark looks thrown our way. "I can't do it. I'm sorry you guys, I can slice him up in a fit of revenge, but I can't sit here and slowly let him go hungry. It's not in my nature."

"And we love you for it," Kingston said. He pecked the tip of my nose, walked around the kitchen island and picked up two plates for our captives. He gave them each a scoop of scrambled eggs with a slice of buttered toast, and that was it. "We don't have to spoil them, this isn't a luxury accommodation or anything, after all."

He flashed a grin and strode into the other room to feed them both.

I wondered if he'd do it by hand so I trailed behind him and watched as he got the plates set up on the coffee table and helped them over to it so they could eat without hands like pigs at the trough.

I can't lie, it felt good to see them like that.

Once again I was proven to be brutally violent at time,

petty like crazy, driven by revenge, but ultimately motivated by love. My Kings made it easier for me to be kind, and that was where I wanted to focus after all this was over.

Kindness over violence.

Although kindness never got me as turned on as violence, I'd have to figure something out.

Because I knew I'd never be normal.

CHAPTER 5

We didn't have to wait seven hours to hear from Ilya, let alone twelve.

I only got a few hours of sleep before breakfast, and afterwards, when I was lounging in the sitting room with a good book, I heard my burner phone ringing from the room next door.

I rushed to it, opened it up and answered it before the person on the other end hung up.

"There she is, the little—" Ilya started to insult me but thought better of it. See? Even old dogs could be trained when their son's life was on the line.

"The little what?" I demanded. I was staring down into the screen, and he appeared to shrink back when he saw my face. "What were you going to call me?"

"The little princess, of course," Ilya replied. He opened his hands and smiled in a conciliatory gesture. He knew I had the upper hand he cared more about Maksim than I did about Ivan and Amara. And it wasn't that I didn't care about them. It's just that Ilya was terrified of losing his son. It wasn't the natural order of things, especially in a crime family like his. He was also afraid of the image it would give, one of weakness. Like he wasn't strong enough to keep his family alive, so how could he be considered powerful and dangerous?

I felt cocky because of this.

"Princess? Okay, because I think I prefer queen," I said. "I'd like you to call me Queen Everly, please."

"What? Don't be stupid, and let's get down to business," Ilya scoffed. He waved his hand dismissively and that just set me off.

"No, you will address me as queen," I said. I had no idea why it meant so much to me at that moment, but I needed more control over the bastard who had almost destroyed my life.

He refused, and we went back and forth for a couple of minutes, when finally somebody said something off camera. It was Russian, so I didn't understand, but Ilya argued. They continued for another minute and finally he sighed and stopped the conversation.

"I've been advised to give into this one demand to show a willingness to negotiate," he said. He was tired. He'd been doing this a long time, running a crime group, but he was definitely hitting that point where he wanted out. I could see the defeat in his eyes.

"So, are you going to?" I prompted.

He sighed again, his weary face dropping from exhausting, and he finally said, "Yes, queen Everly, I'm ready to talk."

"Excellent," I replied and leaned forward, resting my elbows on my knees. "Now we're talking. I want Ivan and Amara by ten tonight, here in London. If you don't bring them, then I'll be slicing Maksim apart, one appendage at a time. Got it?"

He argued with me about the timing, how hard it would be to make it, and even the location. He didn't like the fact that I chose the rooftop helicopter deck of Ivan's building to make the exchange.

Finally, he capitulated. We were done with the debate, and he asked for one more thing.

"What is it?" I asked, disdain clearly dripping from my tone and my expression.

"Do you think there's any chance of a future with you and Maksim?" he asked with hope edging his words. "You'd make a fine member of the family and keep things running smoothly with that sharp mind of yours."

I guffawed and sat up, threw my head back and laughed.

"Not on your life," I replied. "I wouldn't want your family resources or your family problems!"

He was deflated at that, and I shook my head as I ended the call.

Was he insane? I mean yeah, I knew he was clearly nuts, but this was next level even for him.

There was no way I wanted anything to do with his family after this unless it was me running them down on a dark country road or carefully putting a bullet in them where nobody would connect the murder to me.

"Can you believe that shit?" I asked as I slammed the phone on the coffee table. "What would make him think I want anything to do with him or his deranged son after this?"

"I can't imagine you're easy to lose," Kingston said, and draped his arm around my shoulders as he sat on the sofa next to me. "I know I'd make a fool of myself to keep you around."

"I'd do anything," Ryker agreed. "I'd even pretend to like getting fucked up the ass if it meant keeping you around, princess."

"Pretend?" I asked, and raised a brow. "I've seen the way your cock twitches when I'm behind you. I know you like it. We just have to get you used to it from all the guys, now."

I reached for him and grabbed his dick through his pants. It was so bizarre to me, swinging from murder to sex and back again like it was the most natural thing in the world.

But when you craved blood like me, and were surrounded by four gorgeous men, it made sense.

"I'll get him liking it," Archer said. He came up behind Ryker and grabbed him by the hips, pantomiming humping him hard. Ryker yelped and jumped away, but Archer hung on.

"You're a natural," Valen said with a laugh. "We'll get him relaxed and ready to go in no time."

"Not before I have a crack at all three of you," I said. I raised my hand, formed a fist, and thrust it up. Their eyes all widened with horror as I continued. "I have three more I'd like to break in. Oh god, the looks on your faces, like I'm going to use an actual fist. Geeze, you'd think I was out to hurt you."

I laughed, and they joined in. "We're just worried you want revenge for all the things we've, uh, used on you," Kingston said. He looked down at my lap and raised his eyebrows. I knew exactly what he was talking about, not just the dicks or fingers, or even hands. He meant the zucchini. We'd never talked about it, we hadn't had the time, and I was still processing how good it felt.

But I owned it. I could let my freak flag fly with the best of them and still maintain my dignity.

"You know, they say you should have a variety of vegetables in your diet," Valen suggested.

"Fruit, too," Archer added. "Maybe a banana split would keep you full?"

"How about a little meat in there, babe?" Ryker said, grabbing himself and flashing me a wicked grin. "Gotta keep it balanced."

"You guys are terrible," I said, and shook my head, loving every minute of it.

We spent the rest of our time relaxing with each other, ignoring the fact that we had two captives and were waiting to get my father back. Sometimes I had to ignore reality and enjoy what I had in front of me or else I'd go insane.

* * *

TEN O'CLOCK ROLLED AROUND TOO FAST FOR MY LIKING. NOT because I didn't want to give up Maksim and Avery, or because I was reluctant to get Ivan and Amara back. But simply because the entire exchange was going to be so stressful, I didn't think I would be able to handle the way my nerves were already fraying on the ends.

I just knew Ilya was going to try something. And the possibility that one of us would be injured or killed because of it felt imminent and real.

Fuck this whole thing, all because Ilya wanted to force Ivan's hand so he would make more money. All because he tried to force me into marriage, for what reason? To what end? All the shit I'd been through because of Ilya's ill conceived plans started to fester in my heart the more I thought about it, and the nerves began to heal. How could I be this afraid when I was this righteously angry?

"It will be okay," Kingston said, sensing my unease. He rubbed my shoulder to calm me.

We were standing on the roof already, even though we still had five minutes. I wanted to get up there first so I could spot Ilya coming in the distance, to make sure he wasn't dropping down with any other helicopters full of his security team.

"I know," I told him, smiling wanly. I didn't know how it would end up, but I had to believe it would really be okay or there was no point to any of this.

Off in the distance I heard the sounds of rotor blades cutting through the air, but it was London so it could really be anything. Below us the sounds of the street seemed overwhelming, and above us was air traffic, planes taking off and landing in the distance. It was a multi layered city with noise from everywhere.

But in the darkness, I could hear that helicopter and I knew it was Ilya coming for me. Coming to rescue his son and kill us if he could.

As long as he had Amara and Ivan, I didn't care what he had planned. Whatever it was he could try and he would fail.

I hyped myself up mentally, talking myself into a state of readiness as I waited for the helicopter to appear.

And moments later, it did. It rose up over the edge of the building as if he was trying to catch us by surprise, but with Ilya involved, there were no surprises. I was always prepared for anything he'd try throwing my way.

I loved the look on his face when he saw us standing there. He mouth some words and screwed up his mouth in frustration that he hadn't gotten the jump on me or my Kings.

And then his eyes scanned across the rest of us and he found Maksim standing with his hands bound and his head hanging low. I didn't feel guilty about what I'd done, but I did feel a twinge of regret because Ilya might use to to harm Ivan and Amara before he handed them over.

I should have shown more restraint, not left Maksim so beaten down and defeated. Luckily his wounds weren't showing, so at least Ilya wouldn't catch onto his injuries until he had him on the helicopter heading home.

"You'd better keep your mouth shut," I snarled the second

Ilya stepped towards me. "I'm gonna lay out what's happening here, understand?"

His eyes narrowed and then darted towards Maksim. Maksim gave a slight nod and his face pleaded with his father to make this work. Ivan would never be so weak as to beg like that, Maksim was the typical spoiled rich asshole who loved dishing it out but couldn't take it. He crumbled after significantly less than he did to people in his control.

I felt smug knowing he was such a loser, it added a cherry to the top of my nipple slicing sundae.

Ilya glared at me but he nodded vigorously.

"Get Amara and Ivan out here," I ordered. "And you'd better hope they're in good shape or your son is going to pay for it."

I nodded at Kingston who was closest to Maksim, and for effect, jerked Maksim's wrists. Maksim yelped like a dog and cowered in front of us.

"Please, he's going to listen to you," he whined. "He's going to do whatever it takes to get me back."

Ilya ordered Ivan and Amara off the plane and one of his security team ran back to escort them.

"You're getting what you want," Ilya growled. He hated giving into me, I could sense it in the tension carried in his voice and the stiff way he was standing. He was used to being the one doing the orders, not listening to somebody telling him what to do. "There's no need to keep up this charade, you know."

I shrugged and said, "Call it revenge. You could have gotten us killed, and you've had my father and friend for far too long. And let's remind everyone about my professor. You had her killed just to get my attention."

"The professor wasn't me," Ilya replied with anger. "That was Avery and her stupid fucking idea. She's going to get us all killed if she keeps fucking with you, isn't she?"

"I'll do whatever it takes to be left alone," I said and stood closed to him, meeting him eye to eye to assert myself. "Even if it means killing every fucking one of you, I'll do it. If you don't fuck off and leave me alone to live my life, I will come after you. End of story."

Ilya watched me carefully through his constantly narrowed eyes. He was really suffering at the moment, he despised being forced to obey me and I was loving every second of it.

"Fine," he said with a hiss. "We'll leave you the fuck alone as long as you stay away from us."

"No problem there," I said, raising my hands in disbelief. "I was doing that just fine before y'all decided to fuck around. Now you're finding out and you're singing a different tune."

Ilya wanted to argue. I could see a tension tic forming at the side of his temple and he took a deep breath.

Behind him, Ivan and Amara appeared next to one of the guards. They were pretty bad off, both of them were skinny and limping and neither one of them looked like they'd had a decent meal in a long time. But they were alive and they were heading my way.

"Let them go," I called out. "Stay back."

The guard looked to Ilya who nodded his head.

"Come to us," I told Ivan and Amara. "We're in control here."

Ivan's eyes opened wider and despite his gaunt appearance, pride flared across his face.

They shuffled to me, just the two of them, and when they reached me I was hit with a horrible smell. They'd obviously been kept in horrible conditions and were suffering for it.

"Are you okay?" I asked them both without taking my eyes off Ilya.

"I think so," Amara said. "I don't feel anything out of place."

"How about you?" I asked Ivan.

"Better than I've been for a while," he replied and laughed. "Of course you're my daughter, look at you. Who else would have Ilya Kostin eating out of their hand like a tame little pet?"

"She is your offspring," Amara smiled. "She was a little asshole when I told her no, we weren't going to search for you."

I laughed and turned to Kingston. "I guess let them go," I said, indicating Maksim and Avery.

He shoved them forward and Maksim stumbled into his father's arms. Ilya motioned for his guards to help Maksim up, seeming almost disgusted with his own son.

"We don't want her," Ilya said, motioning toward Avery. "She's not our problem."

"She's not ours," Ivan said, frowning. "Why would we keep her here?"

"She's your daughter," Ilya said. "She's your problem."

"She's not my daughter, what are you talking about?" Ivan exclaimed. "Is this what you think? There's no way I'm her father!"

"Well, that changes a few things," I said, a relief bolted through me as I thought about the things Maksim had made us do.

CHAPTER 6

"YOU MADE HER WHEN YOU FUCKED MY SISTER," ILYA SAID IN A low warning tone. "You and she laid together, and my sister came up pregnant. That's the way it works, or have you forgotten how children are made?"

He looked back at his men and laughed. They joined in, but their laughter was forced and nervous.

"I barely knew your sister," Ivan replied. He took a moment as if in deep thought and said, "I don't think I ever spent a moment alone with her."

Avery stood nearby and tears streamed down her cheeks. Again, I was led into sympathy for her. I felt horrible that she was being argued about like a pile of trash. Nobody wanted her. That kind of rejection would be soul shattering.

I couldn't help myself. I walked to her side and put my hand on her shoulder.

"They're all idiots on Ilya's side," I said. "Even if we're not sisters, I feel bad for you."

"Get fucked," she snapped, then her shoulders hunched forward as she began to sob silently. She rocked back and forth on the balls of her feet and made a keening noise, like an animal.

"Thank you," she finally whispered. "This is beyond humiliating. I know who my mother is, but nobody seems to know who my father is. You probably don't know what that's like. You've had Ivan on your side for a long time."

"I haven't, though," I replied. "I grew up without knowing him. I had to live like that my entire life, having a step dad and a half sister by him. Everybody knew about it. They used to mock me constantly."

"But at least you had a dad," she said miserably.

"He raped me," I said matter-of-factly. "I don't mean to be so blunt, but face it, we're not exactly polite with each other, are we?"

She had the decency to look embarrassed. As ashamed as I felt every time I thought about it.

"No, I guess not," she said. "I guess we're way past that now."

"Are you two going to start kissing or are we finished here?" Ilya sneered. Two of his guards were helping Maksim back to the helicopter, and he was glaring at me with such venom I'm surprised he didn't manage to light me on fire right then and there.

"No, we're not done," I replied with disgust. "You've had Avery in your family for years now. Regardless of who her father is, she's your niece and Maksim's cousin. Take her with you. It's the only life she's ever known."

"She's fucking useless to me now," Ilya said. "If we can't make a deal, then what the fuck is the point?"

Faster than I thought humanly possible, Amara was at Ilya's side. She slammed her fist into his temple and reached down to draw a gun from his side holster. She held it to his head and flicked the safety off.

"I refuse to listen to you blather on about another

woman," Amara hissed in his ear. "I fucking refuse to sit here and have you denigrate a girl who has done nothing but obey orders and clean up the filth that you dump on her. You're going to transfer her a million in cash, or I'm going to fucking shoot you right here and now."

"Go ahead," Ilya chuckled. "The minute you try, my guards will unload their guns into you. If I die, then you die."

"At least I'll take you out with me," Amara growled. She caressed Ilya's temple with the end of the barrel, like a dangerous lover. "I'd rather drag your corpse to hell than sit here idly by while you destroy another woman's life."

I wondered what had happened to her when she was gone, because I'd never seen her so enraged. I liked it, but I didn't like that something terrible had to happen for me to see this side of her.

"You don't have the balls to do a damned fucking thing to me," Ilya insisted. "Not after I broke you myself."

Behind them both, Ilya's guards had set Maksim down to the ground and were standing at attention with their guns pointed at Amara. He had six in total, and I didn't see how she was going to get out of this on her own.

Which is why she was lucky that she wasn't all by herself. She had us with her, and my Kings and I had anticipated something like this.

I nodded to Ryker why was standing at the end of the row farthest away from me.

He nodded back, reached into his jacket, and pulled out his own weapon. He snapped the safety, leveled it at Ilya and said, "I guess you'll take this risk over a million dollars? What is that, chump change to you, right? Listen to Amara, give Avery her due, and then get the fuck out of here."

Kingston drew his weapon. Then so did Archer and Valen.

I finally stepped forward, handed Ivan a handgun, and lifted one of my own.

"I guess being around your dirtbag son taught me a thing or two about not trusting anybody from your family," I said with a smile. "I'm sorry about his nipples, by the way."

Confusion flickered across Ilya's face and he opened his mouth then closed it again. He turned around and looked towards Maksim, but his son stood impassive without speaking.He turned back to me.

"What do you mean? His nipples?"He scoffed out the word as if it was a joke. As if he had no idea what I was talking about, and of course he didn't. But he thought it was something amusing, nothing serious.

"Why don't you ask him?" I replied, raising an eyebrow in defiance.

"What the fuck is this bitch talking about?" he asked, turned around to look at his son.

"She hurt me," Maksim said, speaking at last. His voice quavered as if he was about to cry. "She cut me. She made me bleed, daddy. She hurt me bad."

He started speaking in Russian, and tears welled up in his eyes. I was filled with joy at his pain, and I laughed at how he reverted to baby talk when he was fighting humiliation.

After everything he'd ever done to me, this pleased me more than anything else.

"What a fucking pussy," I giggled and waved my gun towards Ilya. "I can see why you wanted me to join the family, then you'd have at least one child who wasn't a complete and utter disappointment."

"It's not that," Ilya exclaimed, whirling back to me. He was still facing down the barrel of all our guns but acting like nothing was out of the ordinary. He was either very stupid or had nerves of steel, and the longer I talked to him the more I suspected it was the first one. "It's that I wanted access to Ivan's shipping networks. It would open my family business up to international destinations we don't currently have."

"You wanted to use them fro drug and human trafficking," Ivan said, narrowing his eyes and brandishing his gun. "Just own up to it. I think that's the worst part dealing with somebody like you. You think I can't see your true intentions because you think I'm as stupid as the rest of you."

"I don't think that," Ilya replied, but you could hear it in his voice. He just assumed we were all as easy to fool as his son and other people he did business with. "Now let's get back to injuring my son. If you did hurt him that much then we demand compensation."

"Give Avery her million before we continue any conversation," Amara said with a sharp nudge of her gun towards him. She made contact with the side of his head and Ilya looked more irritated than pained.

"Fine," Ilya begrudgingly agreed. "I'll do it. Fuck you're persistent."

He pulled out his phone and went through a few actions. I could see him tapping in a passcode, then swiping to send funds, and finally closing it and holding the it up. "Tell the bitch to check her account."

Amara looked back at Avery. "You want to let me know if the money's there?"

I had removed her bonds a while back, but until then she'd been unmoving and almost too stunned to speak. But when Amara spoke, Avery picked up her phone, logged in and waited a few minutes. It always took a little while for money to complete the transfer, and during that time I enjoyed myself by staring down Ilya and Maksim, one by one. Mind games to exert my power and amuse myself.

"It's there," Avery said brightly. "Holy shit, it's there!"

"That should be enough for you to start your life away

from these two losers," Amara said. "Now, go! Get out of here while you can."

Avery nodded, took a step and then another. She looked back as if she was expecting us to be like Maksim and do something terrible to her after giving her freedom. She realized Amara was serious and we weren't going to impede her progress so she moved faster.

She finally bolted out of there, and I heard the door to the rooftop deck slam shut as she pushed her way through.

It was strange to watch her go, and part of me regretted the terrible way we'd treated each other.

But life had taught me to be more pragmatic these days, and I understood that whatever fantasy I had about being her friend would never come to fruition. We were two different people with different lives, and it was best for her to live far from mine.

"Well that's over," Amara said, lowering her gun. "Now get your loser fucking kid out of here and don't cross us again or you'll fucking regret it."

Ilya looked foolish enough to fight back. He had a momentary lapse of reason and squared his shoulders as if he was going to argue.

But he looked at me, Ivan, the Kings one by one, and finally Amara and he thought better of it. He could tell there was the thinnest veil of polite society keeping all of us from kicking his ass, and his son had already been through the ringer with my violent revenge.

Ilya backed away from us, his eyes burning with anger and I knew it wouldn't be the last we saw of him. He'd come after us again, he would have to. He lived by the code of an eye for an eye, but he didn't understand his own part in it. Our damages to him and his family had been reactions to his attempted destruction of all of us. We were reacting, he was acting, there was a big difference.

But sadly, Ilya was too stupid to understand the difference.

We stood still until the helicopter lifted off, and as it grew smaller in the distance, Ivan let out a loud groan and collapsed onto the roof next to me.

Until then, I had thought he'd made it through without issue. But he was hurting, he was just really good at hiding it from all of us.

We gathered around him and formulated a plan get him downstairs and healing again.

It was strange to have him back, but not more strange than having to rescue him.

What a bizarre life I had.

* * *

"Hold still," Amara said as she dabbed ointment onto Ivan's wounds. "This isn't exactly pleasant for me, either, you know. And moving around makes it worse."

"I'm sorry, it fucking hurts," he hissed and writhed under her ministrations. He had been taken care of, relative to the rest of us that was. He hadn't been tortured too much and he hadn't been subjected to starvation or other forms of abuse. He had, however, been tied up most of the time so he had sores on his body from remaining motionless, and his arms and legs were stiff and twisted.

He would need physiotherapy to complete overcome the pain and regain full function. At least that's what the doctor had said when we brought her in to examine Ivan.

Amara, however, would need something more. She had been hurt mentally and physically in ways that I suspected, but hadn't confirmed. I thought she would probably need some time off to take care of herself after this, and I was right. After Amara left us alone, Ivan looked at me and said,

"I've sent her away. She needs to spend time alone to recover. She will be at a wellness spa in Switzerland for a month before returning to the US."

"What are you going to do?" I asked. "How long do you intend to stay in London?"

"Not long," he said and then he paused. "You don't need to stay with me. I understand you have some legal troubles back at college."

"It's a long and stupid story, but yes," I replied. "They started because of my association with you. Avery set me up to get my attention, apparently."

"I'm sorry this opened up such a terrible situation for you," he said and sighed as he relaxed back into his chair.

"What did?" I asked.

"Being my daughter," he said, closing his eyes as he leaned back. "I'm afraid your life will not be easy because of that."

"I think it will stay interesting, I suppose," I replied. There was no sense in complaining about it to him, Ivan already seemed to feel horrible about what had happened. And he was my biological father, there was no point trying to deny it.

"You do like life to be interesting," he said and he opened his eyes to look at me. "What is the story with your friends? I've overlooked it all this time because I thought it was a phase you were going through, but they appear to be permanent."

"You mean my roommates?" I laughed and then grew serious. "They're here to stay. I'm sorry if it feels weird, and I know it must look strange from the outside, but they're my partners."

"Equally?" he asked. "How does that work?"

"I'm not even sure," I said. "It just does."

"Do you have to give them chore charts and keep track of that?" he asked with a laugh. "I can imagine it's hard to get four of them helping out around the house, it's so hard with just one at home."

I joined him in laughter and nodded vigorously. "Oh god, sometimes it is. It's bad enough picking up after one guy, let alone four of them. But I'm pretty mean so I keep them in line."

"You definitely got that from my side of your genetics," he said with a proud look on his face. "Being mean is definitely an asset when you're managing a group of people."

We talked for a little bit until he began to look sleepy. He asked me more questions about the Kings, and seemed to give his approval as long as they treated me well and protected me.

After I left, I got a text from my mom saying she was hoping to see me at Nat's dance recital next week, and if I could let her know how many of my guys were planning on showing up.

It was strange to have something so normal set in the middle of the bizarre circumstances that kept cropping up.

Life would return to normal eventually, but I had a nagging suspicion that this was it. This level of uncertainty was my new normal.

And I didn't know if I was cut out for it.

CHAPTER 7

"THE HOUSE LOOKS OKAY," I SAID AS WE DROVE UP THE driveway of our Oakville mansion. It felt strange to be back in the US and on American soil after being away for over a month.

I'd contacted all of my professors and had called my lawyer to let him know I had returned. He was going to facilitate my negotiations with the police at my college, to help us all work out a deal so I could return to school if my professors would let me.

"The staff I hired could run it on their own for a decade at least before the money runs out," Ivan said with smug pride. "I hire capable people and pay them well from an account that can keep up."

"Not all of us have those abilities," I said, wondering what our house near the college looked like by now. "Maybe I should borrow some for them to keep our place running smoothly."

"Not on your life," he laughed. "I like the way things work for me here. Besides, if I have to admit it, Amara's the one who hired everybody. Now that she's gone for a short time, I need everyone I can get. It takes twenty people to make up for her alone."

"Then I'll steal Amara away from you and you can keep the rest of them," I laughed.

He said no way, and we devolved into a fake fight over who got to keep Amara. If she was there with us, it would have both flattered and annoyed her.

The truth was that we both missed her but were unable to talk about it. We wanted to contact her, but also understood that she needed her space.

I was Ivan's daughter through and through when it came to handling my emotions, so at least we were on the same page with that. Feel them, but deny them, and make jokes with each other to gloss them over.

We stopped in front of the mansion, where the wide marble steps swept down to the paved driveway, and I looked up at it.

I still couldn't believe I owned it. Or more to the point, Ivan bought it for me. It's not like I did anything to deserve it, but it had saved my life and my mental state.

It felt strange, too, to park in front where I'd once climbed in for the prom or where I'd seen my Kings fighting off The Organization to save me. So much had happened here, and yet it still amazed me every time I saw it. It always felt like the first time again, over and over.

I didn't think I'd ever reconcile the two worlds I'd lived in Oakville, between Reg and Mom's place and this one. From my former school to Covington. What a strange life I'd had, from one extreme to another.

And thankfully, despite all the trials and tribulations I'd gone through, I had found my Kings. I would do it all again, even the worst parts, to have the life I led now. With them by my side. I couldn't imagine a world where they didn't rule my heart.

"How does this work, being back?" Archer asked as we stepped out. "Aren't you still wanted for Seymour's disappearance?"

"Our lawyer is on that," I replied. "I don't know if Seymour was ever found, though, we need to look into it."

"I guess we've been a little distracted by staying alive," Kingston said.

"And keeping our prisoners," Ryker said. "Maybe we didn't do so well on that part. How is Maksim these days, I wonder?"

"Probably a little sore," Valen replied. "At least I hope he is, the fucking piece of shit. He has to know he got off easy."

"I hope he's still in a lot of pain." I didn't mean to say it so darkly, but it slipped out that way. I did, too, I hope every time he shifted his body or put on a shirt, he thought about me and the things he'd done to me. I still felt helpless rage when I looked back at my time in captivity, and I still wanted to get more revenge for it. I would have gone back and shot Maksim in the head if I thought I'd be able to get away with it. But I wouldn't be able to get near him now, and if I did succeed I'd only destroy Ivan and Ilya's final thread of business.

Although Ilya had probably already done that, considering the shit he'd pulled by kidnapping him. Ivan wasn't the sort who would forget about it easily, and the small ties they still had in the business world weren't worth enough for him to let it go.

Ilya had to be afraid by now, and rightfully so. One way I wanted to get involved in Ivan's business dealings, no matter what they turned out to be, was to help him take down the Kostins.

It wasn't enough for me to have hurt Maksim like that, there was an itch that I couldn't scratch left over by our abuse. Not only had they hurt me, but they'd hurt my Kings and my father and Amara. For that alone, I couldn't let it go. I wasn't going to be able to rest until I got absolute revenge on them both.

And not just that, the people who worked for them. For the people who had helped facilitate my humiliation. For the guards who had stood and prevented me from getting free. There had to be a way for me to get back at them all, and I would have this itch irritating me until I could get it.

I coughed to alleviate the pressure building in my chest when I thought about the things I would do to them, but it didn't help.

Only hurting them would make it go away.

I wondered if that was a genetic thing I got from Ivan. If he felt the same thing right now, the gnawing need to make it go away.

Was that genetic? I didn't think it was something anybody had studied, or anybody would study, but maybe there was a link. That's why crime and criminal behaviour seemed to stick to families, after all.

"Are you okay?" Ryker asked me when we were inside and heading upstairs. "You seem awfully quiet tonight."

We'd flown in on a red eye flight and it was dark now. I didn't even know what the local time was, my phone hadn't hooked up to wifi and adjusted just yet. It was that strange in between feeling of travel, when you were mentally back in London and also in the US. Like I was in two places at once.

I'd catch up soon, I always did. But for now, I was fully immersed in the strange sensation of not quite belonging anywhere.

"I'm good," I replied. "I think I just want to sleep and then have a huge American breakfast when I wake up. The bacon never tastes quite right overseas."

"Or the coffee," Ivan agreed. "I'll give our staff the head's up, they'll be ready for us."

We agreed, and I finally padded upstairs to my bedroom. My Kings followed close behind, but none of us were in the mood for sex, we were all too exhausted. I wanted to express myself sexually now that we were home, but not yet.

I needed sleep and comfort more than I needed an orgasm.

I know, can you believe I was saying that? It's almost like I had matured or something.

Or perhaps the captivity and torture had caused me to reevaluate what I needed from my guys.

None of it mattered, though, because I dove into bed and they followed. Soon enough we were curled up like a nest of lovers under the blankets, our limbs entwined and our bodies seeking comfort from each other even when we slept.

It was more than enough for me, and exactly what I needed.

* * *

"THIS IS EXACTLY WHAT I WAS TALKING ABOUT." MY MOUTH was full of bacon but somehow I managed to get the words out. The bacon was perfection for my undernourished body, fatty and salty and full of flavor. The breakfasts we'd had in London had been delicious, I mean the English knew how to make it a big event, but there was ultimately nothing quite like home.

"Oh yeah, have you had these pancakes?" Ivan asked me while stuffing his own face. "Mrs. Nelson can make them so freaking fluffy it's like eating a cloud."

"A cloud dipped in butter and syrup," I said with a laugh. We were the only ones awake and were indulging before anybody else joined us. A true father and daughter moment where we realized we were more alike than we ever knew.

"You know what would be even better?" Ivan said and he raised his eyebrows.

"What's that?" I asked.

"Bacon and pancakes after killing the Kostins," he replied and slipped a piece of pancake into his mouth.

I sipped my coffee and inhaled the scent. "I agree. That would be delicious and satisfying. But would it be possible?"

"Maybe not us," he replied. "You have school that's more important than taking down our enemies. But eventually we could, or have somebody else do it."

"If we have somebody else do it, would that be good enough?" I asked him, and I wondered that myself. Would we be satisfied just hearing about it, or would it fulfill something inside of us even if we just directed it.

"It is, from my experience," Ivan replied, and then he paused with his fork up and a piece of pancake on it. The sunshine was coming in through the windows around the breakfast nook and it illuminated his hair from behind. It was like a halo, but I could see even more grey hair around his temples and in his short beard. "It's more than enough to simply know you had a hand in their demise."

"Are you okay with that?" I asked, making sure he wasn't making a mistake. "Because I could wait. In fact, waiting might feel better because they wouldn't expect it."

"The whole revenge is a dish best served cold thing, hey?" he asked with a chuckled before eating his pancake.

I could see him savor the flavor and I wondered how much we looked alike. I could see myself in him sometimes, but most of the time I thought I just looked like me. People said I took after Ivan more than my mom, but who knew? People were known to be wrong.

"Something like that." I laughed quietly and felt embarrassed suddenly. I always felt like there was a part of me trying to impress Ivan. As if I was afraid he would be disappointed with me and would withdraw his support and money if he found me lacking. It was stupid, and I knew it was stupid, but I had that constant pressure inside my stomach about it.

Maybe I wasn't as vicious as I assumed, maybe I was just trying to make Ivan proud with my murdering violent urges.

Then again, he hadn't been on the scene when I'd taken the gun, aimed it at Reg, and pulled the trigger. That had been one hundred percent me. All Everly Hayes, and not Evie Popolov.

"Yo, did you leave anything for us?"

Kingston's voice burst into the nook ahead of my boisterous, energetic Kings and everything shifted immediately when they sat down. They began to talk about the food and their night, and even the fact that they wanted to go target shooting in the large training center behind the house later on.

I looked at Ivan, raised my eyebrows, and we laughed together. Not because we were laughing at them, but simply because we both knew they balanced us. Like Amara did with Ivan when they were alone, my Kings kept both of us real and settled, or else we'd drive each other into intensity and violence in no time flat.

Without my Kings, we'd both be lost.

CHAPTER 8

"WE'RE MEETING WITH OUR LAWYER THE MOMENT WE GET into town," I told Ivan as we loaded up our luggage to head home. We were going to fly and would be there in a couple of hours. I didn't know what to expect, we didn't have the staff to handle the house when we were gone and we hadn't heard anything about the charges against me.

"You make sure he keeps you away from the cops until they guarantee your freedom," Ivan said. "If he fucks up and you end up in jail again, he's going to hear from me. And I promise, he's not going to like what he hears."

"I believe it," Archer said. He was serious with a grave expression on his face. Ivan scared him on some level. Hell, he scared each of them on some level and I liked that.

"We'll do our best to keep her out of trouble," Kingston reassured him. "We'll be there every step of the way."

"I'm sure it will be cleared up today, if it isn't already taken care of," I told Ivan. "It will all be behind us and I can beg my professors to let me catch up."

"I told you, if any of them give you any trouble at all just let me know. Everybody has a price and I can talk to them for you," Ivan said.

I cringed at the image of him sending them big stacks of cash to bribe me backing the program, but at least I had a backup if they turned me down based on my begging.

We said our final goodbyes and climbed into the SUV that would take us to the airport. We were talkative in the car, but not about anything worthwhile. Just sexy talk, them complaining about getting their own classes back, and then the dirty things we were going to do to each other when we were finally alone in our own home.

The pilot was waiting for us on the tarmac and we exited the SUV, leaving it for somebody to drive back to the mansion.

"Welcome," he said and helped us with our luggage. "We don't have a flight attendant for this one, but I'll do my best to get you there in comfort."

"Oh my god, how will I survive?" I playfully rolled my eyes and picked up my own suitcase. "It's okay, I'm sure we'll be okay during the two hour flight."

It was still funny to me that this was my life now. I had gone from never being on a plane to having the pilot of a private jet apologize for not having somebody to wait on us hand and foot.

The flight went off without a hitch, and we were back at Fincross before we knew it. There was no police presence waiting for me at the airport, which was a good sign, but my lawyer, Thomas Paquette, had sent a car to pick us up.

He still didn't have any news, good or bad, about my case. I was all nerves and jagged edges as we made our way home. Driving past the college left me feeling sick to my stomach. I looked up at the tall main hall and the towers on the science building and a wave of nausea flooded through me.

It wasn't enough that I might be able to go back here, if I

was able to beg my professors and get back in. It was going to be awful as long as Seymour's fate was unknown. I assumed Paquette hadn't told me about her because there were no answers.

Avery knew, she was the one who had done it. That much was obvious even though she'd never outright admitted it. I regretted letting her go, I should have shaken her and gotten the answer from her before rewarding her with the money from Ilya.

"It's going to be okay," Archer said, leaning against me and looking over my shoulder at the buildings beyond. "My father has already talked to my profs and I'm back in."

"Me too," Valen said. "It's just been a month and it's not exactly hard when dear old dad offered up some cold hard cash to have me slipped back in like nothing happened."

"Must be nice," Kingston said. "I don't have a rich dad, I don't even know where mine is."

"I know where mine is, but he probably owes money to some crack dealer," Ryker said with a grim laugh. "It's not like he'd help me even if he did have the cash or the influence."

"Ivan offered but I said no," I told them. They turned to me, incredulous, and I continued. "I know, I should have taken the help but I thought it would be better if I tried to do it on my own. I'm stupid and stubborn I think."

"Not stupid or stubborn, just wanting to get things done on your own," Ryker said.

"Hey, I don't know about Stubborn. I could get behind stubborn, because holy shit, you know how she is when she gets her mind set on something," Archer said with a laugh.

"Okay, stubborn in certain ways," Valen agreed.

"Yeah, like when she's horny," Ryker agreed. "Remember? She wouldn't leave me alone until..."

"We all know about that, we were there, dude!" Kingston

laughed loudly and clapped Ryker on the shoulder. "We saw the whole thing, you were like no, no, it hurts, I can't, don't stop, harder, harder, baby!"

That left us wheezing with laughter and Ryker was red faced but enjoying it as much as us. He was embarrassed because it was true. He'd gone from being reluctant to being a complete and utter butt slut.

I had to stop laughing when I thought about the nature of my stubbornness, though. Was I just punishing myself somehow? Why didn't I use Ivan to get me back into school? I wasn't as poor as Ryker or Kingston, but I'd grown up like them. Maybe that's why I still clung to my fierce independence even if it might cost me my schooling.

"I'll get Ivan to speak for you two," I told Ryker and Kingston. "It's not fair that you have to suffer because of my family. It's not right."

"Your family?" Kingston asked, seemingly hurt. "I thought I was part of that family, princess."

"You know what I mean," I said, suddenly shy at his declaration. I always thought of them as family, my husbands even, but had never said as much. "I mean Ivan. I'm sorry you guys got dragged into Ivan's fuckery."

"We didn't get dragged anywhere, we do whatever we feel like," Ryker told me. "You should know that by now. We aren't exactly timid creatures waiting for you to tell us where to go, we go where we want to."

The car pulled into the driveway of our college mansion and I instantly felt exhaustion and stress leave my body. It felt like home at last, somewhere to let my hair down and let my Kings take care of me.

We thanked the driver and dragged our luggage to the front door. Archer took mine, so I only had to drag my ass as we walked slowly. The grass was overgrown and there were flyers and bills stuffed in the mailbox at the front door. The front veranda desperately needed to be swept and there were leaves piled in every corner, from the wind blowing them around.

"It's not as bad as I thought it would be," I said, withdrawing my keys. I clicked one in the lock and opened the door, stepped in and almost fell to the floor as the month away caught up to me all at once. My legs felt boneless and I could barely hold the keys in my shaking hand.

"That was so fucking intense," I said and exhaled loudly. Tears formed in my eyes and shook my head. "Did that even just happen?"

Flashes of the torture and capture haunted my head and I couldn't escape some of the images. The worst being Avery, of course, and Maksim's gun against my head. I didn't know how long it would take for those images to disappear forever, or if they even would.

"You okay, babe?" Ryker asked as he sidled over to me. He dropped his suitcase and wrapped his arms around me. "You look like you could use a hot bath and something to eat."

"I need that," I said. "And I need to fuck. I need sex to alleviate this persistent feeling that I'm about to explode. I need us all to reconnect again, I crave it."

"I get that," Ryker said. He kissed the top of my head and held me like that. Kingston, Archer and Valen joined in, the best group hug in the world. My Kings surrounding me with their tall, muscled bodied, their collective masculine scents, the press of them holding me, and the safety of their support and physical presence.

I didn't know how women did it with just one man, that felt strange to me at this point. I knew society would judge the hell out of me for being like this, people would call me slut or freak or many other things, but the way I felt between them all was the most natural thing in the world to me.

I wouldn't have it any other way.

* * *

"You realize you've been gone for a month and you were implicated in the disappearance of one of your professors, Miss Hayes," Fincross's dean of students told me over her desk. She was an older woman with a mass of grey curls and kind brown eyes behind wire framed glassed. She was looking over them at me and I put on my most pleading face to appeal to whatever goodness she had in her. "This application to rejoin is going to be a tough one to handle."

"I understand all that, but we have a family emergency in Europe and it was a matter of life or death. I could get my father in here to discuss it, but I'm trying to do this on my own. And you might notice that I've been cleared of all suspicion in Miss Seymour's disappearance."

"Yes, I did see that," she replied and narrowed her eyes as she looked me up and down with suspicion. "I don't know how you will handle this academically, though. You've missed so much."

"I think you'll find I'm an eager learner with a quick mind," I told her, leaning forward to look into her eyes. "I really, really want this, and I'll do anything to make it happen. I can catch up in class by doing extra work in the evenings and on weekends. I'll make school my top priority."

"I'll take it to the board and we'll rule at tonight's meeting," she replied, and sorted some papers on her desk. "I can't say with any certainty that the board will got either way. You'll have to wait until tomorrow."

"Thank you," I said, standing and extending my hand. She took it and I shook hers vigorously. "Thank you so much, that's all I'm asking for. A second chance without me using my father to buy my way back in."

She nodded and said, "I'll have my secretary call you for

72

an appointment tomorrow. If that's all, then I have work to do."

I nodded and she was done, she dismissed me by taking some of those papers and sorting them before writing something on the top one. While she was busy, I quietly stepped around the chair and left her office.

Her secretary smiled widely as I passed, and I said, "I'll be hearing from you tomorrow. I can't wait!"

She nodded and waved as I left the dean's office.

God, that hadn't gone as badly as I thought it would. I'd found out that morning that I'd been cleared of any wrong doing in Seymour's disappearance. Apparently she was still gone, but I just wasn't a suspect anymore. Sandy had been the one who had stopped by to tell me, and her entire demeanor was so different than when she had been interrogating me at the police station.

She'd suddenly been contrite and friendly and even asked me where I got my jacket, as if she loved it so much she just had to run out and buy one herself.

It had been an interesting turn of events, I had to say. But it didn't solve one thing, and that was where Seymour had gone to.

That one still haunted me, it drove me to constant distraction as I went through everything I'd said to her that drunken night, and everything I knew about the case. Sadly, that was almost nothing. I just knew she was gone, and even though all evidence pointed otherwise, I felt guilty for it. Maybe Avery had done something to get my attention, maybe Seymour had been so hurt by my horrible rant, or maybe I'd just been the proverbial straw that had broken the camel's back. I couldn't shake the feeling that it had something to do with me.

"What'd she say?" Kingston asked as he loped to catch up to me. I was just leaving the main administration building and he'd been waiting for me. The others were dealing with their own classroom stuff, but Kingston had already been to his one class of the day. Much to his surprise, all his professors had welcomed him back.

Not to my surprise, though, most of his professors were women who seemed to get pretty flirty when he was around. And the one male prof was gay and flirtatious with my King. I loved to see it, though, him using his hot self to get ahead. Not that I'd ever point it out, to him it was just normal, the way things have already been done by women, so why not him?

"They have to rule tonight," I said, feeling stressed and dejected, not a great combination.

"Then there's only one thing for us to do," he replied. "It's time for a night of distraction and relaxation, and you know what that means."

He nuzzled my neck, nipping playfully as he slid his hands down my ass. I giggled and tried to twist away, but I was trapped.

"I know exactly what it means," I said in between gasps of laughter. "It means we'd better make sure we're stocked up on lube."

He made a low growling noise, and I realized at once that I wasn't sure who it was for. Me or him or all of them.

But I couldn't wait to find out.

CHAPTER 9

"Catch!" Ryker called out and tossed a cherry tomato at me. I grabbed it in mid air and popped it in my mouth. I was sitting across the kitchen island from him as he prepared dinner. The four of them were doing their best to keep my mind off the ruling meeting tonight, and food was always a good start.

They spoiled me in this aspect, I was well fed and well fucked by them all. Just another reason to let my satisfaction settle in on my heart. I had always been afraid to let myself feel it, because it had always felt like I was attracting bad luck. But lately, especially after coming back from Maksim's, I felt more comfortable leaning into my good luck. My good life. All the blessings and riches that I had, because without them I would have succumbed to the darkness years ago. I would have ended my miserable life, or become a deeply unhappy person.

I was finally learning to love what I had, and allowing it to brighten my mind.

Sometimes I felt like a frightened animal slowly being

coaxed into domesticity. Step by step, being brought into their loving arms.

"You're getting good at that," Kingston said from where he was tenderizing the steak he was about to take outside and grill. "I guess you like things in your mouth."

"You, of all people, should know that," I grinned and reached for another tomato. I brought it to my lips and sucked it slowly, letting him get a good look before putting it inside my mouth. I enjoyed his immediate reaction as his mouth fell and his eyes widened.

He shifted and I knew he was hard, I could tell just by the look of him.

"Come on, we're never getting dinner done if this is the way we're talking," Archer complained. "Unless you want me to find another zucchini, that is."

"We might have one in the fridge, I'm pretty sure I picked one up at the store yesterday," Valen said, raising an eyebrow. "I know Kingston threw in a box of condoms just in case we want to use something interesting on you, princess."

I gasped and my chest felt hot. The heat creeped all the way up to my cheeks, but also all the way down to my throbbing pussy. As much as I had that immediate effect on them, they did the same to me. The moment they said something overtly suggestive, I was lost to them.

"Well, I mean vegetables are supposed to be good for you," I said and blinked, looked down, and then scanned across all of them as demurely as I could.

"Fuuuck," Kingston exhaled. "I'm not getting these cooked, am I?"

"You'd better turn off the grill," Ryker said, flipping the dial on the stovetop to turn it off as well. "I think we're gonna be turning on the girl instead."

I groaned at the dad joke, but I was ready. I needed what they were offering, I craved it bad.

"We gonna fuck her with a vegetable this time?" Archer asked as he stepped around the island towards me. "Or are we gonna just do it with our dicks? Because right now, I'm on team dick."

"I'd like to vote for dick, too," Valen said, adjusting himself in his grey sweatpants. "I'm all about team dick right now."

"I'll add my vote for team dick," I said with a laugh and I turned around on the stool to face the four of them as they approached me like hungry predators. "I'll vote for four of them in particular, in fact."

Kingston moved first. He'd abandoned the steaks, washed his hands, and headed my way at the first mention of dick. He swept in and kissed me hard, his tongue entwining all slippery and sensually with mine as his hands groped at my body.

Archer was next, being the closest to me. He leaned over and kissed my exposed neck and fondled one of my breasts. On the other side, Valen did the same, kissing my shoulder and playing with my earlobe between his fingers.

I was wearing a tank top and little skirt, I'd been thinking about going to play tennis with Neve later, but I would have to call it off because I was going to be busy. She'd been ecstatic that I was back, and thrilled that I was free. She was dating two men herself, now, and was wanting to talk to me about adding a third.

I would have to suggest she added one more after that, because it felt like the perfect amount to me.

I groaned and felt Ryker drop between my knees. He pushed them apart and the other men moved out of the way to give him access to my hot, waiting pussy. He tugged at my panties and slid them over my hips and down my legs. He inhaled my scent off them and tucked them in his pocket. He was such a hoarder of dirty underwear, mine of course, and I always wondered what he did with it until I walked in on him in his room one day. He had a fist wrapped around a pair of my panties and was jerking off with his other hand, rubbing my panties up his cock shaft every few strokes, then bringing them to inhale my scent as he masturbated.

It had been so hot, and so unbelievably flattering that I was obsessed with watching them jerk off now. Maybe tonight would be the night I demanded they all do it in front of me, for my enjoyment.

"Fuck, you smell good," Ryker grunted and put his hands on my thighs. He pushed them farther apart and I moved my ass until I was on the very edge of the stool.

My pussy was exposed to him and he used his thumbs to pull my lips apart so he could get a good look at it.

"You're so beautiful down here," he exhaled in reverence. "I fucking love looking at your pretty pink cunt, princess."

"She's a delicate little flower," Valen said while kissing my neck. "I love it."

They each extolled further virtues of my pussy after that, but Ryker's mouth made me forget everything they said the moment they said it.

His tongue lapped at my juices and flicked my clit while his lips made me feel like he was french kissing me as hard as Kingston was working on my mouth.

Archer dropped to his haunches next to him and reached under my thigh to press his finger into my soaking wet, waiting entrance.

"She's so fucking tight," he rasped and slid deep and fast. "I love the way she feels from the inside."

The two of them somehow worked together in time, licking and sucking and finger fucking me with skillful agility. They were the synchronized pussy attack team and I was their victim, gratefully, their willing receiver. If eating and finger fucking a pussy was an olympic sport, these two would have the gold.

I groaned and writhed on the stool but hands kept me in place and their movements kept me from falling off. Kingston let Valen kiss me, stepping back so his friend could cover my mouth with his and swirl his tongue endlessly around mine.

It didn't take long, it never did with that first orgasm. Just being around the four of them in our regular lives had me vibrating on a higher horny frequency than normal. Our usual playful banter always had that background of flirtation behind it, and I was basically ready to thrown down into sex at any given time.

I truly believed if I had just one boyfriend, I would have either worn him out or scared him off by now. I had too much to contain in one person, I had to share my hyper arousal with four of them to even it out.

I felt the familiar pressure in my core, the fluttering in my pussy and the heating up in my body that indicated I was about to drown under a wave of pleasure. I twitched and clenched my walls around Archer's fingers, and sucked Valen's tongue hard to hide the sounds of my yelping bliss.

And then as the crescendo rose, it finally hit its peak and crashed down again. I cried out, Valen pulled back, and the four of them touched me, stroked me, fucked me, and licked me until my cries turned to triumphant joy and my orgasm left me in a shuddering, weakened state.

"It's time to get you upstairs and properly fucked," Kingston said, kissing my forehead. Ryker kissed my thighs to my knees and stood up, sweeping me into his arms before anyone else. Luckily, Archer's finger was long out of my pussy or they might have fought over who did the honors.

Kingston took me up the stairs while the other three followed. We left dinner uncooked on the counter so we could come back down later and finish it. We'd need the nourishment after an epic adventure into sex.

We went to my room, the one with the largest bed and all the toys. And lube, plenty of lube.

Kingston set me on my feet at the end of my bed and the four of them stripped me down. They joined me by tearing off their clothes, and at long last the five of us were naked and ready for whatever the moment brought.

"I want to fuck you, princess," Ryker said, his face still shining wet with my juices. "I deserve the honor of fucking that hot little cunt."

"Only if I get some," Kingston said, stepping behind his friend. "Fair play, bruh. You know you've had me more than we can count, I think it's my turn."

"I think it's all of our turns," Archer said, running his hand down Ryker's hip. "You've fucked each one of us raw a few times now, I think it's time for payback."

"I approve," I laughed and climbed onto my bed. "As long as I'm getting stuffed, I think there should be enough for everyone."

"Fine," Ryker said, seeming reluctant but I knew him well enough by then that I could tell his hard on was that stiff because of me, but also the anticipation of being fucked at last. He'd been our last hold out until I'd taken his anal virginity, and now it was my other Kings' turn. Ryker had fucked each one of them over the past few years, many times even, and yet he'd always played hard to catch.

Tonight was the night we were going to catch him. All of them, that was, because I wanted him inside of me. There was nothing hotter than being fucked by two men on top of each other. IT added a heft to the thrusts that felt more solid, more depraved somehow. Like they were pushing through and getting me in places a single man couldn't get to.

Ryker climbed onto the bed with me, and the other three

men followed. Kingston watched closely as Ryker covered me with his body and kissed me hard until he slipped his fat, pierced cock inside of me. Kington's eyes lit up as Ryker began to pump.

"Hold on a sec," Kingston said after a few minutes of it. Archer handed him some lube from the nightstand and Kingston generously drizzled it all over his shaft and Ryker's crack.

He tossed it to Archer and positioned himself behind Ryker. I looked up at Ryker and caught his eye, smiled and brought him down for a kiss.

His cock was throbbing inside of me, and I clenched hard to reassure him. He was nervous, but he was so fucking horny his eyes were almost wild with it. Like he was an untamed horse finally being broken to ride.

Kingston went slow, pushing past Ryker's unused tight ring with a gentleness that surprised me. He and Ryker were usually so rough with each other, rivals often, more so than with anybody else. I expected Ryker to fuck Kingston hard the first time, but I supposed he hadn't, really. And I definitely expected Kingston to go wild on Ryker's ass, but he was so smooth and kind, it was endearing. The love we all shared for each other extended into our sex and made it that much more special.

"Fuck," Kingston exhaled slowly, his favourite word while fucking. "You're fucking tight, relax, Ryker. Take a deep breath and loosen up."

"It feels weird," Ryker said, but his cock twitched as Kingston spoke to him. "I want to like it though. I know I will."

"Just let it happen, babe," I whispered to him and brought him closer for another kiss. He kissed me so hard my lips hurt, and when Kingston finally thrust forward, Ryker's teeth grazed my lower lip, drawing blood.

That didn't stop us, though. We kissed through the iron tang of my bleeding flesh and the painful stretching of his tight asshole. Kingston picked up speed and that in turn slammed Ryker into me, and I came hard almost immediately. When Ryker came, I went with him, and so did Kingston. The three of us together was magical, pure wild sex magic. It was healing and bond making, bringing every one of us closer as we came.

Ryker's gift was staying hard even after an orgasm. Archer took Kingston's place and was soon fucking Ryker's ass like a pro. He gripped Ryker's hips and covered him like a stallion, leaning over with his tall height, close enough to kiss his back.

He came quicker than Kingston, but he'd been ramped up pretty hard. It was to be expected. Ryker didn't come that time, but I did. I think I didn't stop coming, it was all so beautiful and sexy.

Valen climbed behind Ryker after that, and beside us, Kingston and Archer began to kiss each other and work up to full on fucking so they could join in.

I was in heaven, cocks everywhere, men everywhere, and all the love in the world at my fingertips.

Valen went slower, more sensually with Ryker and Ryker appreciated it. I could see it in his eyes and in the soft way he moved on top of me. Kingston and Archer moved up the bed, and stayed on their sides. Kingston got behind Archer and I saw him slipping lube up and down his shaft before he slid inside my lover.

Archer looked down at me, curved over and began to kiss me until Kingston started to fuck him from behind. Archer straightened out, as tight as a drawn bow, and gasped.

His hard cock was close to my face, so I pulled him across the landscape of the bed until he was close enough to suck.

Kingston fucked him up the ass, I sucked Archer's cock,

Ryker was buried deep inside of me, and Valen was deep inside him.

It was absolute sexual perfection, and I had never been so filled with love and bliss and ecstasy.

I never wanted it to end.

But of course, human bodies need fuel. So after a couple hours of this, trading places and positions but making sure we were all well fucked at the same time, we grew exhausted.

We wandered back down to the kitchen in search of sustenance and finished our meal some time long after midnight.

No matter what happened in my life, that would stand out as one of those perfect moments to hang onto until the day I died.

I just hoped I had many, many more.

CHAPTER 10

I was called into the dean's office first thing in the morning. My knees felt weak and my hands were shaking when I drove to the college and I wished I wasn't alone.

My Kings all had left for school an hour before I got the call. They were diving back into their studies, but I was waiting to find out my future.

If only Avery hadn't dragged me into the situation with Seymour, I could have slipped back in with minimal consequences. Even if Ivan didn't advocate for me directly, everybody knew who I was. Everybody knew I was loaded, and could cause a world of trouble if I wanted.

They didn't know I wasn't like a lot of kids who had grown up with wealth, I didn't use it as a weapon. In fact, my money still made me feel slightly embarrassed at times, ashamed to be rich now when most of the world still struggled to survive.

I always felt like I hadn't earned it, so I didn't deserve it. Maybe I'd get over that once day, but for now it wasn't helping me deal with my current situation.

I'd even used Ivan's influence to help Ryker and Kingston, but it hadn't helped me so far.

When I got out of my car, I closed my eyes and took a deep breath. I was trying something new lately, focusing on the positive instead of getting tangled up in the negative thoughts that always took over my head. I knew it wasn't going to change my life or anything, I wasn't one of those 'manifest your destiny' types, but I was tired of being scared all the time.

And that's what it boiled down to, my anxiety was driven by fear. I'd lived in that state for so long that it had become normal for me. When I wasn't afraid, I was waiting for something to happen. It was as if I was constantly holding my breath, and that left me exhausted and anxious a lot of the time.

I was tired of feeling like that, so I'd read online that focusing on the good in my life might help. It needed to center myself before big events like this, so that even if it didn't go my way I wasn't going to let the blow to my fragile stability send me spinning out of control.

I guess that's what it was mainly about. I was tired of feeling like I was just balancing on the razor's edge. On one side was violent madness where I used my money and power to fly to Austria and gun down the Kostins like the dogs they were. Where slit Maksim's throat instead of merely slicing his chest, and I shot Ilya after making him watch.

The other side of that was the one I pursued now, with my deep breathing and positive affirmations. That was the side where I gave mercy and sought peace. I wouldn't ignore the world's problems, but I wouldn't let them consume me. I could do more people more good if I took care of myself and the Kings first and then worked outwards from there.

I could help when I found abused people, I could destroy when I found bullies.

But I wouldn't make that my entire mission, I wouldn't spend my life looking for horrible people. I could spend my life looking for victims and giving them some relief, that would be enough.

"Are you okay?"

I opened my eyes and realized I'd been standing there for an awkwardly long time. Neve had caught me like that, I didn't know how long she'd been in front of me as I'd stretched.

"Oh," I laughed nervously. "You caught me. I was just trying to psych myself up to go find out the results of last night's meeting. To find out if I'm allowed back in."

"I wish Seymour was found so they'd get off your back," she said. "I mean, the cops cleared you even if that one bitch was being a total twat about it."

Neve had gotten more outspoken now that she had two boyfriends. Although she's been on the way on her own, I liked to think I had something to do with it.

"That's basically what my friend Penny said," I replied and laughed. "You two would get along."

"Does she have more than one?" Neve asked, raising a single eyebrow. I got her drift.

"No, she's firmly attached at the hip to her one and only true love," I said. "It's cute, actually, they're like one complete person when they're together. They're very happy."

"So I'm your only wild friend like you?" she asked with a sly smile on her face.

"I guess so," I replied and joined her in letting out a small laugh. "I never thought about it like that, though. Like there's us and them, I feel like everybody just figures out what fits and goes with it."

She looked stricken and her face fell. "Oh my god, I'm sorry," she stammered. "I didn't mean to imply there was something wrong with your friend. I was just trying to be goofy, to take your mind off things."

"No, I didn't mean it like that," I said and waved my hand as if sweeping away any negativity. "I'm sorry if I came off as a condescending asshole. I just meant everybody is entitled to their own lives, and I don't want people to think that I'm judging them for anything. As long as it's consensual and safe, then people can do what they want."

"I didn't mean to make you feel like you had to apologize," Neve started to say and then laughed louder. "Fuck, I'm such a dork. I can't even talk about having more than one boyfriend without sounding like a total creeper. Clearly I'm not the wild friend here."

We talked it out a little more, and I realized Neve was just trying to be accepted with her new lifestyle. I understood that feeling, the pressure of needing to fit into society's narrow standards and the need to escape them. Neve was feeling what I'd gone through in the beginning, when I'd felt like a slut at one moment, and a liberated queen the next. Like I was simultaneously better than, and yet worse than everybody else.

The human brain was so stupid sometimes, the things our own thoughts put us through.

The alarm went off on my phone and I took another deep breath to center myself.

"Well, this is it. Time to find out if I slink off with my tail between my legs, use Ivan's money and power to bully my way back onto campus, or they decided to let me come back," I said.

"I'll walk with you. Give you whatever support I can."

I thanked her and meant it. Having anybody by my side was so much more meaningful than I thought it would be. It was unexpected and something I didn't realized would help until I had it.

I just wished the Kings could have been there with me, too, but I did understand why they weren't.

We walked across the grass towards the main administration building and I was once again awed by the tall turret towers and classic architecture of the building. It was the quintessential college campus, it oozed money and privilege, and had the air of sophistication that hid all of the drunken frat parties and casual hook ups that happened on its grounds.

Fincross was elite and not for everyone, but it was just like the rest when it came down to students behaving badly.

"Okay, this is it," I said as we reached the front stairs. "I'm ready to find out, wish me luck."

"Do you want me to come up with you?" she asked, looking towards the dean's office on the third floor.

"No, that's okay. I didn't even expect anyone to be here now. It helped more than you could imagine," I replied.

She watched me walk up the steps and when I got to the landing, she walked away towards her class. There was no way I felt comfortable having Neve sacrifice her classroom time to sit and listen to my fate being determined by those who were fully entrenched in their academic life. It felt strange to have a bunch of privileged people with their careers in full swing telling me whether I was going to have a future at Fincross or not.

I put my hand on the front door handle, squeezed and pushed it to walk inside.

I heard my name being called across the lawn and let go to turn around.

And I found my four guys running towards me, tumbling like four puppies with their long limbs and tumbling, chaotic energy.

My heart zinged with delight and love flowed through me.

"Everly!" Kingston called again. "Wait up!"

Valen was first, being the fastest, followed by Archer, then Ryker and Kingston taking the stairs two at a time together.

"I thought we missed you," Valen said with a breathless voice.

"We left our study hall," Archer told me, breathing heavy. "We were supposed to be there another hour to prove that we're serious about reintegrating into the semester but we couldn't leave you alone."

"You need our support, princess," Ryker said and he reached over my shoulder to push the door open for me.

"We'll be waiting for you," Kingston said. "Good luck, I hope this goes well for you and we don't have to bring out Ivan as the weapon."

"Imagine weaponizing my father against the school," I chuckled. "I almost hope they turn me down so I can see him come in here and kick ass."

"They won't," Archer said, kissing my forehead. "Now get up there before you're late!"

Valen and Ryker each slapped my ass as I left and I grinned the entire way to the third floor.

The dean's office had a reception area, and the secretary told me to take a seat.

"Is this about the board meeting last night?" she asked me as I sat near her desk.

I nodded, unable to speak without tears choking my throat shut. I hadn't realized how scared I was until I got up here.

"Good luck," she said. "I hope you get what you want, they're all in good moods lately so that might help."

"Thanks," I croaked out and then looked down at my phone to pass the time.

I didn't even chat with Penny or the Kings, all of them were texting me like crazy demanding play by plays of the entire thing. I didn't want to, because I worried I would break down if something happened, and then I'd blurt it all on text. I needed to maintain my composure no matter the outcome, so I would tell them later.

The worst thing I could do would be crying in front of them. I wouldn't give them the satisfaction.

"Miss Hayes, she's ready for you," the secretary said, standing up and indicating the door to the dean's office.

I walked through and prepared myself to hear my fate.

"Hello, please have a seat," the dean said, gesturing to the same chair I was in the day before.

"Thank you," I said and sat down, but on the edge of it. Literally the edge of my seat as I waited for her to talk.

"As you know, there was a board meeting last night and your case came up," she said and gave me a kindly smile. I felt more relaxed at that, why would she smile if she was about to destroy my world? I nodded and she continued. "We discussed all aspects of it and looked at your previous work. Your grades are normally excellent, which helped."

I nodded and let her speak.

"And I am pleased to let you know that if you join the catch up sessions with your friends, then you will be allowed back into Fincross to complete your studies. There's nothing we can do about Dr. Seymour's class, though. You failed your midterm before you left."

"I understand," I said and fought the giant grin that threatened to take over my face. "Thank you so much, you don't know how much this means to me."

She nodded and again gave me a kindly smile. I stood, we said our goodbyes, and I yelled the results to the secretary as I ran past her desk.

"Congratulations!" I heard her call to me as I hit the top of the stairs.

I didn't know I could jump that fast, but I took the stairs

down two at a time. I ran out to where my Kings were waiting and told them the news.

"I'm saved!" I exclaimed and let the laughter bubble out of me. "I'm allowed back in and I have to come to class with you!"

They surrounded me, kissing me and hugging me, holding me and lifting me up with their kindness and love.

And from that moment, it felt like everything was back on the right track again.

Of course, like everything else in life, the moment I was up simply meant there was room to go down again.

And of course, it happened sooner than I expected.

CHAPTER 11

"Y{\scriptsize OU} {\scriptsize KNOW THIS MEANS CELEBRATION}," K{\scriptsize INGSTON} {\scriptsize SAID}, draping his arm across my shoulders. I tucked into him, soaking up the heat from his body and letting the joy of the moment wash over me.

"And what do you mean by celebration?" I asked, of course, my mind going straight to sex.

"We're taking you out. Not now, though, because this week is going to be our crack down week," Ryker said. "We have to kick ass and catch up."

"After that, we were thinking of a short trip away," Valen said. "Maybe just a couple of nights in Vegas?"

"Or would you prefer a spa getaway?" Archer asked.

I loved it when they inundated me with choices, but sometimes they all came at me at once and it was over-whelming. As if being overwhelmed by love could be a bad thing.

In my new spirit of positivity, I decided to let it go, and lean into their love. Normally I might feel anxious about trying to please them all, or scared that I would hurt somebody's feelings, and so I would let myself drown in their desires to make my life better.

But now, in my new attempts to alleviate stress and fear, I let it lift me up like a little feather on the currents of a river. I floated happily along, letting them talk around me about all the different options we had to escape the vigors of college life.

Because in the end, all that mattered was that I would be somewhere with my Kings. And I would be getting railed good and hard by each and every one of them.

But then, as I relaxed, I felt an urge shine through the jumbled excitement and I knew where I wanted to go. I actually wanted to lead the way and make a decision.

"Vegas," I said with a sudden exclamation. "I want to go to Las Vegas. I don't want to hide from the world anymore. I want to go somewhere we can be our wild and outrageous selves and nobody will notice a thing."

"That sounds perfect, princess," Kingston said, and he raised his eyebrows. "You realize if we go to Vegas, we get to take you dancing, right?"

"Of course," I said and laughed. "Wait, why? How did you make something as innocent as dancing sound so dangerous?"

"Because all four of us will surround you on the dance floor and we'll make you our sexy queen for the night," Ryker said, as his eyes grew distant, thinking about the scene.

"I think I could handle that," I said and dramatically put the back of my hand to my forehead. "If I'm forced, that is."

We were still at Fincross after my meeting and needed to get back to the make up classroom. The college had been persuaded by our wealthy families to provide a TA and an empty room to give us study time. We had to catch up in each class individually, but most of the professors were being very accommodating and allowing us projects instead of doing each assignment on its own.

This was good news for me, especially when I realized how many small tests, reports, and essays I'd missed during my absence. I couldn't quite understand how I'd been so lucky to have supportive teachers, but it felt like my luck might be changing. The winds were shifting and I might just have good things coming my way at last.

We got set up around the table in our private room and got to work fast. There wasn't any point in talking or fooling around, not when there was work to be done. That being said, I couldn't help myself from time to time when I would reach my foot out under the table to slide it up the leg of one of my Kings.

There was something so powerful and thrilling to see them shift and look my way with pure, hot lust in their eyes.

Sometimes when I was extremely bored and needed a brief mental break, I would push my foot up higher until I found the hard ridge of their cock straining against the fabric of their pants. There was something especially powerful knowing that simply being near me was enough to keep them hard and ready at all times.

It didn't take long to breeze through the assignments I'd missed and write the short essays to make up for quizzes that had happened while I'd been away.

We left in the afternoon and headed for home. My lawyer had given me a list of advice to follow until the police found out what had happened to Seymour, and number one was to travel between home and school and nowhere else.

He worried that if I was seen having dinner or out with my Kings, it would trigger people or the police into thinking I was living a fabulous, full life after Seymour's disappearance.

Because of this, Vegas was a fantasy, but something I

could look forward to. I needed those lately, little goals in the future to help me through the intensity of the past month. I would make it through and leave all the negativity behind, time did heal all wounds as everybody said. Until then, I would occupy the silent spaces in my head by dreaming of dancing in public in a wild place like Las Vegas instead of letting myself get pulled down by the reality of Fincross. The tension I felt by being the main suspect in Seymour's disappearance.

"What are we making for dinner, and more importantly, whose turn is it to load the dishwasher afterward?" Kingston asked as we were sitting around the kitchen table doing homework a few hours after getting home.

"I think the real issue here is how we're gonna talk you into doing it again," Ryker said, narrowing his eyes, looking Kingston up and down.

"That's what I want to know," Archer agreed.

Kingston looked over at Valen and me. "You two want me to make dinner, too? Is this some kind of conspiracy happening here?"

I held his gaze until I felt a smile tug at the edges of my mouth and I couldn't hold it in any longer.

I burst out laughing and said, "I think it's obvious that it's Ryker's turn to clean up but yes, I would like it if you'd cook. You're the most talented by far."

It wasn't a lie and it wouldn't hurt the other three Kings by me stating the truth. Kingston could make anything taste like high end restaurant, he had a gift. The problem was that we took advantage of him maybe a little too much and he would get irritated at times.

Kingston sighed, rolled his eyes and pushed his chair back onto two legs. He was very dramatic about accepting his place as the best cook, but he loved it.

He dropped back down, sighed again and said, "Fine. I'll

cook. There's this roasted tomato sauce recipe I've been dying to try out but I'm not cleaning up a fucking thing. That's on you, dude."

He looked at Ryker who did his own dramatic response by sighing and rolling his eyes.

"Fine. I'll clean up. As long as I get to fuck our queen later without you trying to get at my ass. That's my one demand of the day."

"But you like it when I get in there while you're in her," Kingston said with a pout. "At least I thought you did."

"I do, but I'm still sore from the last round," Ryker said, straight faced. It was still wild to have food smoking hot guys talk about sex out in the open like that. Knowing they enjoyed being with each other now, almost as much as they enjoyed being with me. I never felt jealous of their plans, I understood what they needed the roughness of fucking each other and with four of them, it never took attention from me.

I didn't think I'd ever get tired of seeing it, too. There was something so powerful and feral about hot, muscled men rolling around with each other. Especially knowing that I was their prize. I was the one thing they all ultimately wanted at the end of their grappling each other.

They agreed on their terms and Archer and Valen sat back, amused at the constant give and take between the two dominant Kings. Archer and Valen were happy where they were at, neither of them had anything to prove and they were equally content with the love and sex they got whenever they needed.

They were also better suited to being with each other, they'd fooled around before they met me and now I gave them the freedom to explore whatever they wanted.

They weren't as prone to the rough ass fucking that Kingston and Ryker got up to, but they were more into the sensual oral that always sent me over the edge into oblivion. They would give each other head or bring me in so we were a triangle of pleasure. Sometimes when Archer was fucking me, Valen would eat his ass, or vice versa.

Fuck, just thinking about it was getting me so wet and hot I began to think dinner was off the table. I would be on it, getting devoured and fucked by all of them.

And then my stomach rolled, demanding I eat, and it won. I could put off my hunger for sex some times, but right now my pussy didn't stand a chance. I was starving.

"I don't care what you cook, please start soon," I said, looking down where my stomach let out another unhappy grumble.

Kingston's eyebrows raised and he laughed as he stood up. "Right away, my hungry queen."

"Maybe we could feed her while you're busy cooking," Ryker said, raising his brows as he looked me up and down.

"What do you—"

I was about to ask what he meant, but his eyes let me know.

"Oh, that," I said with blush creeping to my cheeks.

Ryker began to clean up his textbooks and worksheets, Valen and Archer followed suit.

Kingston tidied up before getting into the kitchen, watching us from behind the counter as he started our meal.

"What are you doing?" I asked as Ryker packed up my books and cleared the table of anything.

"I think you know, princess," he said and reached down to put his hands around my waist. He lifted me up unto the table, gently lowered me down, and kissed me as I laid there with my legs dangling over the edge.

He kissed me harder as his hand moved between my legs and lifted my skirt. He pushed my thighs apart and I felt other hands join his.

Archer and Valen helped him as positioned himself in the V of my legs, sat on my chair and pulled it forward. He was the perfect height to kiss my pussy as he leaned forward.

I moaned as he spread my lips and dabbed his tongue against my slit and my clit.

I felt swollen with heat and desire immediately. Like an overfilled balloon, about to burst. I was ready to gush and I wanted him to touch me more, to eat me harder.

"Fuck, this is hard to work while you've got her spread out like that," Kingston said from the island where he was working on dinner.

"Get over here and get her ready for us," Ryker said, pulling back. "I'd love you to flood her cunt before I eat it."

"You're such a fucking pig," Kingston said, but his voice was thick with desire. "And I fucking love it."

He stepped out from around the island, his hands down his pants already. I watched as he walked towards me, pulling the waist of his sweats over his massive hard on. It popped out and bobbed straight out in front of him, a single eyed beast ready to impale me on the kitchen table.

"Oh yeah," I groaned and watched Ryker move out of the way so Kingston could come in hard and fast.

"Oh yeah, princess," Kingston said with a cocky grin. "You know I can't concentrate when I know your little cunt is begging for me just a few feet away."

"Fuck her," Valen said from one side. "Fuck her hard, I love seeing you slam into her."

"She can take it," Archer agreed from the other side of me. "She loves it, don't you? Tell us how much you love it, babe."

"I do," I said with a breathy voice that was bordering on being shaky. My pussy was clenched in anticipation and the deep heat of desire was roiling in my stomach, replacing the hunger pangs. "I love it. I love all of you so much, I love your love and I fucking love your cocks."

I felt Kingston position himself against my entrance. His cock head pressed hard and began to split me open, that first moment that I never forget but always managed to excite me. The first contact, the first inch inside. It was always exquisitely intense and filled with the sensation of lust and love.

"I love you and I fucking love this," Kingston breathed out and thrust forward. His cock plunged into me, filling me up and throbbing against the walls of my clenching cunt. "I love this so much, Evie. I love you."

"I love you too," I gasped and waited until he bottomed out before relaxing. I let his slide back, then slip forward again. He pulled away and slammed back in, now that my pussy was slick with heat and juice. "Fuck, I love you."

He fucked me harder then, and the other three encouraged us with words and their intense observation. It was empowering to have an audience when I was writhing on the end of a cock, I felt like a porn star, like their golden little baby and their lover queen.

I came quickly, as if on cue. It took him given me a deep dick move where he slowed, ground his hips against me, and twisted his hard cock inside. The way it made me feel complete and full of him, the connection it gave me through the pulse of his throbbing shaft, and the quiet sensuality of the moment were all too much.

I let go, unraveled and cried out as I bore down, fluttered my pussy along his dick, and let myself sink into orgasm.

He joined me, spurting his hot seed against my womb with a great, long, deep groan of release.

"Yes," he grunted and finished with one short, sharp thrust. "Fuck, yes."

"Yes," I sighed and felt empty the moment he pulled out. "Yes, and yes, and yes."

I laughed, feeling so good that I was almost lightheaded, and watched him push his softening cock back into his pants.

"I'm gonna get dinner going while I enjoy the show," He told me, dipping down to kiss me passionately. "I always love watching your face when you come, princess. I love you so much."

"I love you too," I said, and no sooner did I say it, Ryker took his place between my thighs once more.

"I love you," he said, looking down at me. "And I love that moody bastard over there. And these two. We've got a good thing going here, but right now I want to eat your little cream pie."

I arched my back and opened myself up to him. He pulled the chair back, sat down and began to lick the hot mix of Kingston's seed and my soaking wet pussy juices from my throbbing slit.

"That feels good," I said and let my body relax once more. "It feels so good."

"It looks good from here," Archer said, reaching over to cup the mound of my pussy. "Fuck, it looks good."

He moved his hand up to my breast, and Valen worked on the other side. They pushed my shirt up and began to play with my nipples as Ryker went to town on my cunt.

It was so much and so perfect that I came quickly. As I tightened up my body, twisted against Ryker's demanding mouth, and cried out his name, he slipped two fingers inside of me.

He fucked me, licked me and brought me to another orgasm as he lapped hungrily at our mixed fluids. It was hot and sensual and I couldn't get enough.

Luckily for me, there was always more to come, I never had to go without.

THE MOMENT I FELT RYKER'S FINGERS SLIP FROM MY PUSSY, Valen took his place between my legs. The moment I felt Ryker's fingers slip from my pussy, Valen took his place between my legs. He sat upright and watched as his fingers slid inside of me.

"This is fucking hot," he told me, looking up with his eyes shining. "Two fit inside you perfectly."

"Try three," Archer said, his voice deep and demanding. "She can take it, can't you?"

I nodded, desire taking over any sense of logic. I wanted him to stretch me open, I wanted him inside of me.

Valen did it, he fit another one inside and pushed as far as he could.

"That's hot," Ryker said, watching with his face in a serious mask of concentration. "Do another one."

Valen looked up at me and I nodded vigorously, not trusting myself to speak. I didn't want to beg him for it.

He slipped four fingers inside and I was stretched so wide it made me nervous, but I loved it. I wanted more, I wanted him to fuck me hard like that, but his thumb kept getting in the way. I moaned and spread my legs, let Archer suck my nipple while Ryker began to roll the other one in his thumb and forefinger. I was overwhelmed with desire and madness for more. I gasped and said, "More. All of it."

Valen's eyebrows raised and Ryker grunted his approval. He loved to push everything to the extreme, he was always trying to test our boundaries and he would be on board with this.

"What's going on over there?" Kingston asked from the kitchen. "Are you doing what I think you're doing?"

"What do you think I'm doing?" Valen asked with a rasping tone.

"Fisting her?"

"Then yeah, bro, I'm doing what you think."

"Oh fuck, I"m not gonna miss this," Kingston said quickly. I heard the oven door close and he tore his oven mitts off as he rushed over. He got close to my pussy and said, "Oh fuck, this is hot. Fuck her, Valen. Put your whole hand inside."

"You sure you're okay with this?" Valen asked me, and I nodded vigorously. Now that it was on my mind, it was the only thing I could think about. I wanted his whole hand inside of me, like I'd seen online in pornos and pictures. I'd always been freaked out by it, but now that he was this far in me, I wanted more. I wanted it all.

"Okay, princess," he said and let out a small groan of pleasure as he worked his thumb carefully into my entrance to join his fingers. Within moments, his entire hand was in me, with his fingers and thumbs all smooshed together into a point. He twisted and pushed slowly, gently, with love and care.

I loved him for that. As much as my feral instincts wanted him to fuck me hard and tear into me, he knew there was safety to consider above all our animalistic pleasure. I loved that they all took their time to make sure I could handle what they were doing.

I groaned and I didn't recognize my own voice. It was so raw and savage, a noise I'd never made. The four of them were so focused on my pussy where Valen's hand was disappearing that I took a moment to look at each of them to ramp up my bliss.

They were all so fucking hot, and so filled with lust that I could practically feel it rolling off them.

I arched my back as Valen twisted his fist inside me, then pulled out. He slid back in and soon had a rhythm going. I was being fist fucked, and it was the strange and hottest thing I'd ever felt.

I groaned again and again, panted like I was running a race, and felt my pussy flutter and clench Valen's fist over and over. We developed a rhythm of slow fucking, and I could imagine his cock as hard a rock and desperate to get inside of me.

"I can't handle this," he rasped and reached for his dick with his other hand. "This is so fucking hot, I can't handle not coming with you, princess."

"Let me help," Archer said, pulling Valen's cock free of his pants. "I need to do something."

"Me too," Kingston said, reaching for Ryker. "We could help each other out."

I watched as Archer worked Valen's cock, Kingston grabbed Archer's thick shaft in his hand, and Ryker moved behind Kingston. I felt like I was in a haze of sex, a wild fuck fest of hormones and animal urges, and I loved it. Ryker lined himself up and slid inside Kingston and began to fuck him from behind, while Kingston jerked Archer's cock. Archer, in turn, jerked Valen as Valen was wrist deep inside of me.

It was crazy hot, and I came within minutes. But it was an

orgasm unlike anything else I'd ever experienced. It was all consuming, like a wildfire razing a forest, burning it up and leaving nothing in its wake.

It was so intense it almost hurt, and I loved it, it felt crazy good but I knew I couldn't do this that often. It had to be like a celestial event when the stars aligned and everything felt perfect. I wasn't about to get fisted every day.

As soon as I began to come, the Kings joined me. Valen spurted thick ropey cum into Archer's fist, Archer came into Kingston's grip, and Ryker came buried balls deep inside my King, my first love.

Valen pulled his hand out of me and I gushed fluid over him and the table.

"Oh god, I made a mess," I exclaimed in horror. I was embarrassed, it wasn't like I'd done it on the bed, having it on the smooth wood surface made it so much more obvious.

"Never be ashamed for being a sexual creature," Kingston said, heading back to the kitchen for paper towels and cleaning spray. "Now, if we left it for the housekeepers to clean up that might be something to be concerned about."

"Oh god, can you imagine?" I laughed, mortified but grateful my Kings were all so cool with everything we did when it came to sex.

"I'm sure they'd be begging to join our little gang of sex," Valen said, helping Kingston clean up under me. Archer and Ryker helped me off the table and onto my feet. I looked for my panties that had been ripped off at some point and saw them hanging from the back of a dining chair across the table. I had zero recollection of that happening and smiled to myself when I saw it.

"Don't you mean gang bang?" Archer asked. "Isn't that what this is?"

"I think more like a bang gang," I laughed, heading around the table for my panties. I slipped into them and tugged the edges of my skirt down to my knees once more. My pussy still ached and throbbed from the fisting just moments before, but already it felt like a distant memory. "A gang bang means you're all banging just me, and from what I've seen that's definitely not the case around here."

"That's a good point," Kingston said, swiping the table one last time. "You're probably right. We're lucky to have such a smart little queen, aren't we, boys?"

Anybody else who would say something like that would come off sounding like an insincere dick, but Kingston meant it. They all did. Every King agreed with him and looked at me like they were proud to be with somebody like me.

Each one of them operated under the belief that I was perfect and I could do nothing wrong.

It's not like I wanted to prove to them that I could be a colossal fuck up from time to time, but the pressure of them thinking I was perfect was unusual for me to experience.

I wasn't perfect, not even close, but their loyalty and belief and love did help me feel close to it at times.

I grinned and reached out to smack his ass as he walked past and said, "You know I am, you boys are lucky."

"I know you're being ironic, or somewhat self deprecating," Ryker said, coming up behind me. He wrapped his arms around me and nuzzled the back of my neck. "But we mean it. You are pretty fucking amazing from where I'm standing and I know the guys feel the same way. I want you yo believe it about yourself. To feel as good as we think you look."

"I do," I said with a smile. I felt his love wash over me. "Especially right now, when we're at home with just us. I love times like this."

"Me too," Ryker said, murmuring with his lips brushing the skin on the back of my neck, raising the hairs there as a shiver passed through my body.

We helped Kingston with dinner after that, and at one point he stopped and said, "If I knew that's all it took to get you all over here to get dinner faster, I would have demanded we fist you more often."

I giggled and wiggled my hips. "Well, we'll see. There are many more meals to prepare and many more years for us to experiment."

"If that's the case, then count me in," Ryker said, taking my hand and kissing it.

"Me too," Archer replied, raising a single brow. "I'm here for the long run, babe."

"I don't need experimentation to stick with all of us," Valen said with a low tone indicating the strength of his emotions. "I just need you. You're the reason I'm here and the reason I get up in the morning."

"You know why I'm here, Evie," Kingston said, putting down the dish he'd been wiping with the drying cloth.

"Why are you?" I asked, prodding him to open up.

"I'm here because you're my first love and my only love. I don't need anything but you to keep me by your side," he said.

"That's all I need to know," I said looking around at them. "I love you all, and I love what we have. I want us to be here for the long run and I wanted to know that we all feel the same way."

They all agreed, nodding their heads and reassuring me that this was it. They were here for life.

It felt good, not that they had reaffirmed it, but that they understood my need to hear it. We couldn't ever legally recognize our union, as unconventional as it was, but knowing they felt the same way that I did gave me the sense of security I so desperately needed.

We finished cooking, then eating and washing up. It was such a domestic scene compared to the wild sex we'd had earlier in the evening that sometimes I couldn't quite reconcile our lives. They felt so normal and even boring at times, and yet at the drop of a hate I could be kidnapped or fisted on our dining room table.

What a strange world we lived in, and how I hoped it would tilt more and more toward the steady, predictable life I wanted to lead with them.

After everything else, we went to bed and I dreamed of being surrounded by muscles and love all night. It was perfect, as perfect as they saw me.

We had another couple of fantastic days like that. We were able to ignore the world and live in our little cocoon of happiness and joy. We would go to school, attend classes, meet for our catch up assignments, and rush home right away. There was something drawing us back together, to our house so we could be alone and away from the whispers and stares on campus.

The worst was when I was alone, going to and from classes or just sitting in the lecture theaters. Neve helped me in the places we shared, in the classes we took together. She kept me distracted as people talked and that helped me ignore the way they looked at me like I was guilty.

It nearly drove me crazy at times, the weight of their suspicions, but I wouldn't let them get to me. I couldn't let it happen.

I knew the truth, that Avery had something to do with Seymour's disappearance, at least I thought she did. She had taunted me with it, and claimed to have set me up. Hell, even one of their men was in the jail that night with me so I did believe her on some level.

But what if she had just seen an opportunity and taken it?

What if Seymour had been harmed by somebody else?

It worried me to think about one of our fellow students being a killer, but after everything I'd been through, I knew that anything was possible. Anybody could have a dark heart no matter what they looked like from the outside.

I wondered how hard it would be to find out. To trace Seymour's last night and discover what had happened to her.

Maybe I could do something to find out the truth and end these glances of suspicion and whispered rumors so I could enjoy my learning in peace.

Back to that boring life I wanted so badly.

"What are you thinking about?" Neve asked, leaning towards me at our lab table. "You look like you're planning something serious."

"Maybe not that serious," I said with a laugh. "I was once again wondering what the hell happened to Seymour and how I could figure it out. I can't stand all these people watching me all the time."

"You know they're just assholes," she whispered harshly. "They don't know shit. If anything, they're more interested in your relationship with the four hottest guys on campus. Now that's been the talk of everything lately."

"I hope so, I'd rather that than Seymour."

"I promise, they think you're a big old slut and not a murderer," she insisted.

I grinned, nudged her and said, "Thanks. That means a lot, you know."

"You're welcome," she giggled. "I never thought I'd ever be praised for calling somebody a slut."

"These are strange times," I said. "Strange times indeed."

She nodded sagely and we carried on with our experiment, talking and ignoring everybody around us.

Thank god for small miracles and good friends in the middle of the chaotic world at large.

CHAPTER 13

"Your investigator called," Kingston said when I got home a few days later. "He said he's on the right track and will update us at the end of the week."

I'd done it, I'd hired a private investigator to find Seymour. I ran it past my lawyer and had talked to the cops, and even the ones who despised me and thought I was guilty agreed it wasn't a bad idea. They were stretched thin and lacked the resources necessary to finish the case so any information would aid them in clearing the case.

I guess boring middle aged female college professors disappearing wasn't top priority for them. Now if she'd been some beautiful young mother or even the daughter of somebody famous, they would have made it their number one case.

But now, Seymour had dropped off the radar for the police in our town and nobody seemed to know anything anytime I called.

"Thanks, babe," I said and tossed my backpack on the dinner table where I'd been railed hard earlier that week.

I still thought about it every time I took a seat at the spot where I'd been fisted. I was fascinated by the image in my head and the memory of the sensation. I wasn't ready to try it again any time soon, but it was still in the back of my mind quite often.

It had been a singular defining moment in my sexual exploration, and I couldn't ignore it or forget about it that easy.

"Hey, babe, remember we're going out tonight," Valen called to me from the rec room. "We have a business major's department dinner. It's just for bullshitting and making connections, so no pressure."

"I do," I said. "I have a dress picked out already, and have we decided which one gets to be my boyfriend for the night?"

Valen appeared and looked over at Kingston. The two of them shared a look and he said, "We all do. We've decided to share you for the first time at college."

"We're tired of hiding it," Kingston agreed. "None of us feel good lurking around in the shadows, so why wait until Vegas? We want to show you off now, and here where people know us."

"I need guys to stop trying to set me up with their sisters and other women they know," Archer said, joining us. "I hope if they see us together then they'll fuck off with that already."

"Oh I'm sure they'll want to keep you far from their sisters and friends if they see the five of us together," Kingston said with a laugh. "I'm sure they might even consider keeping themselves away from us, too."

"I don't want to lose you business connections," I exclaimed in distress. "Maybe we should keep everything on the down low after all."

"Princess, I don't think anything is on the down low anymore to begin with," Ryker said from the rec room with Archer. "Besides, I'd rather not give anybody money if they're going to judge us like that anyways."

"Good point," I replied and relaxed. "Okay, life is coming together. We're going to be out on campus at last, and the private investigator is going to completely clear my name once and for all by finding Seymour himself."

"Sounds like everything is going well," Archer said. "Ilya and Maksim have been dealt harsh blows by Ivan's supporters, too. I heard they've had to leave Austria and flee to Russia in the middle of the war with Ukraine. They have no money left."

"Isn't that dangerous?" I asked, opened my eyes wide as I imagined the two of them dealing with bombs and fighting.

"It's very dangerous," Kingston told me.

"Then, good," I replied as I narrowed my eyes, extending my imagination to them being shot down in the street like the dogs they were. "Very good. I'm glad to hear it."

"There's our girl," Ryker laughed as he joined us in the kitchen. "Now go get your gorgeous self in that dress you picked so I can imagine tearing it off you later."

"Or sliding it up over your hips and crawling underneath it," Archer said. "I love getting a good taste before you've had a chance to shower."

"It's the best vintage," Kingston agreed. "Nothing better."

"You guys are nasty," I laughed, but I loved it. Nothing about my body bothered them, not even when I was on my period or bloated and feeling awful about myself. They saw nothing wrong with me ever, and did their best to make sure that I knew it. "I'm going upstairs to get ready, and you all had better keep your hands off me until after the dinner. I don't want to show up with smeared makeup and messy hair."

"You mean the 'just fucked' look?" Valen asked with a cheeky smile.

"Exactly," I replied. I sashayed away from them, feeling eyes burning into my ass as I walked. Again, I loved the fact that they were all so horny for me no matter what I felt like. I could do no wrong in their eyes and it bolstered my confidence and helped my fragile ego toughen up.

As long as they loved me, I could do anything.

I went over the top for my appearance, I wanted them to be proud of me and I wanted any haters to be jealous of my looks. Sometimes I could see how beautiful I was, when the mirror wasn't warped by my own self criticism. I looked a lot of Ivan, and not in a masculine way. My eyes were tilted at the edged and my cheekbones were high. So despite me having kind of a baby face with chubby cheeks, my face still looked angular and beautiful.

No matter how much I worked out I'd never get rid of that baby face, though. I was sure I'd appreciated it once I hit my fifties and above when all the skinnier girls looked older and I maintained my innocent appearance.

I couldn't even imagine being that age, and I couldn't imagine what my life would look like. I prayed I'd still have all four of my Kings, and I prayed that we were all still happy together.

I'd never thought a lot about children or whether I wanted them. I'd taken care of Nat for so long that it felt like I'd already been a mother at times. Maybe I could get a dog or a cat if I had the urge, I worried about the world and bringing a child into it might make it worse.

What if I couldn't keep them safe from people like Ilya and Maksim? What if the Organization got their claws into my child? The thought of it was maddening.

I shook my head and scattered all my anxious thoughts into the wind as I sat at my mirror in my dressing room. I had an island in the middle of all my clothes where I would apply make up and do my hair.

I was so spoiled now compared to how I'd been living with Mom and Reg. Sometimes when I looked around at the nice things I had, I felt like it was still a dream. As if I'd wake up back in my old bedroom with my shabby second hand items bought with my babysitting money.

I finished my makeup and hair with some time to spare and took a moment to admire my work in the mirror. I'd gotten so good over the last couple of years, I could hardly recognize myself compared to the mousey girl I'd once been.

I shimmied into the dress, a red sparkling Chanel sheath with diamond straps, and listened to my Kings in other parts of the house.

I loved moments like this, where the place was quiet except for the muffled sounds of them horsing around, joking, wrestling, listening to music or playing video games.

Sometimes I felt like a den mother to the rowdiest pack of boys, and sometimes I felt like Tinkerbell with Peter Pan's lost boys, eternally flitting about to care for their every need.

And that's why it all worked so well. They cared for me and I cared for them. I had enough love and lust to spread around, never giving any one of them too much at the expense of the others. I always had a sense when one of them needed a little extra attention or something special done for them, but never to the detriment of my other Kings.

It was an intuitive gift, something I was proud of. My skills at managing our family were a source of great pride for me. It wasn't something I could put on a resume, but I could hold it tight in my heart.

"Evie, are you almost finished?" Kingston called out as he walked into my room. He skidded to a halt when he saw me with my sharp cat eyes, red dress, and swept up hair with delicate curls framing my face. "Fuck, you're beautiful."

The way he said it was a declaration of love and approval. Everything that needed to be said about me.

"What's taking so long?" Ryker grumbled as he joined us,

but the moment he looked up he stopped next to Kingston and his jaw hung open. "Christ, what perfection."

Archer and Valen came tumbling in together after them, their matching khakis and pressed white linen shirts looking like they stepped out of a fashion magazine.

They joined in with the others and looked at me with dazzled, overwhelmed expressions.

"I take it I look pretty good?" I asked, and wiggled my ass at them as I turned around with my hands out like I was a game show hostess. "Is this what you had in mind?"

"Perfection," Archer nodded. "Absolute perfection."

They all agreed, so we headed out to the car that was waiting for us. On nights we were going to drink, we always took a car service. It made sense.

It felt strange, though. I hadn't felt much like going out since we got back, and especially with Seymour still missing. I was hyper aware of the face that so many would see my actions as uncaring or irresponsible. But I was also hyper aware that hiding out all the time would give off the appearance of shame.

And I had nothing to be ashamed of. Not my love, not Seymour, nothing at all. I wasn't just proud of my relationship, but I was proud of everything I'd done in my life up to this point.

The driver pulled up in front of the Fincross's Emerald Club, a high end club reserved for the elite among the elites. In this case, it meant business majors and their guests, most of the other departments didn't have the kind of money the business kids did.

Kingston got out, held his hand for me and I stepped onto the sidewalk. I was immediately bombarded with people greeting my Kings with excited voices and I immediately felt like a third wheel. Or a fifth leg, I supposed.

"I think this is one of those times I'm glad I'm not a business major," Ryker said, standing close to my side as we walked into the club. "It feels like a cult or something, all these people worshipping the all mighty dollar."

"They're just excited, they haven't had time to host any decent events in the past year or so," I said. "Let all the Chads and Tiffanys have their night."

"I've never met a Tiffany that I liked," I said, frowning in concentration. "That's so weird, you know. Not a single one."

"Same goes for Chad," Ryker chuckled. "They're all major douche bags with the most punchable faces."

"I thought most people had punchable faces where you're concerned," I teased.

"Not in our little bubble, but outside of it? Yeah, I suppose so," he smiled at me. He still had a little scar above his left eyebrow from one of the fights he'd been in back at Oakville. It would stay with him for life but it fave him character, it added to his bad boy aura.

"Well, let's get this done," I told him and we stepped through the doors into the dazzling ballroom where I was so glad I had worn my Chanel. Initially I'd been worried that I had overdressed, but once I saw how decked out everybody was, I felt a little under dressed. I didn't have a real mink stole draped across my shoulders, for one. And I wasn't clutching a fifty thousand dollar Birkin bag, for another.

Man, these business kids knew how to spend money. Thank god we had enough to fit in.

"There's the most beautiful girl in the room," a voice said behind me.

I turned to find my three other Kings with Brett Blackstone. Brett, another name I didn't care for but he wasn't such a bad guy from what I remembered.

"Uh, thanks," I stammered and looked to my guys for help. They knew what was bothering me, so they stood around me as if to guard me. I just didn't like making small talk, especially with men I didn't know.

"You're not only beautiful, but you're useful, you know," Brett said, lifting a glass filled with clear alcohol towards me as if toasting me.

"In what way?" I asked.

"You got blamed for Dr. Seymour's disappearance," he said, and his words slurred together, meaning he was drunker than I thought.

"Why would you care about that?" Ryker demanded, standing taller and looking at the other man.

Brett seemed to wake up for a moment. He shook his head and his eyes focused on me.

"It wasn't anything," he said, his cheeks flaming red with heat. "I was just talking out my ass. Now listen, Ryker, if you decided you wan to invest, remember to come to me."

He clapped Ryker on the back, and Ryker tensed up immediately.

"What the fuck did you mean about Seymour?" Ryker demanded again. "It sounds to me like you know something about her disappearance. If you do, then fucking tell the cops about it so they lay off Everly here."

"It's okay," I told him, trying to sooth his temper and ease his mind despite my own curiosity. Why had Brett Blackstone mentioned Seymour, and why did he mention it in association with me?

I talked my Kings down in their anger, then went into a quiet corner to text my investigator.

I had the right to know what part they played in all of this, and he would be the one to find out.

Until he got back to me, though, I couldn't do anything about it. So I decided to enjoy myself and so whatever I wanted with my Kings.

Polite society, be damned.

CHAPTER 14

to our table. "Are you okay? Blackstone is being a complete
fucking asshole about Seymour."

"I sent a message to the private investigator and I'll let
you know if he gets back to me," I told them and took my
seat. I picked up my wineglass to pour myself a drink, but
Ryker tipped to bottle towards me and filled it for me.

"What are we gonna do about it, though?" Valen asked, his
brows curled together in concern. "We need to tell somebody
about this."

"There's not much we can do. The cops have made it
obvious that they don't care anymore and my lawyer won't
be able to talk to them unless we have concrete evidence," I
said. "About all we can do is have a good time and follow it
up tomorrow."

I raised my glass expectantly and they didn't disappoint.
We clinked our various drinks together and made a toast.

"Here's to having a good time tonight, figuring out this
Seymour business tomorrow, and living our lives in happi-

ness beyond that," Archer said, taking the lead. "And as always, here's to Everly and her perfect little pussy."

"Oh, I can drink to that!" Kingston chuckled.

"Come on, can we just do one group speech without mentioning my vagina?" I giggled, but I was flattered. They were obsessed with it, and they were in love with me. That's all I could ask for.

"You know we can't," Ryker smirked and raised his glass again. "To the prettiest little pussy I've ever met."

"Wait, how many have you met?" I exclaimed with fake jealousy. I was territorial, not jealous. The difference was that I trusted my Kings, I just didn't trust anybody around them.

"The only one I remember is yours, princess," Ryker said, flashing me a lopsided grin.

"Good response," I said and sipped my wine. "Excellent response, really. The only one I wanted to hear."

"I know you well," he replied and raised his eyebrows. He licked his lips slowly and his tongue was hypnotic as I imagined it sliding across my clit, drawing an orgasm closer to the surface with each pass. God, he did know me well.

As I was staring at him, the music changed to a new song that I liked, and Kingston stood up. He held out his hand and said, "We have to dance."

"I don't know, I might need more of this," I replied, tilting my wine glass from side to side.

"Drink fast, princess, we're gonna dance," Ryker insisted.

I drained my glass and stood up, swaying as the wine already hit my head. I was such a lightweight but I knew how to keep it so I was just a little tipsy now, not over the top like the night with Seymour.

"I want a dance, too," Kingston pouted as we began to walk away.

"Then come out with us," I said, turning back and

extending my hand to him. "Let's really give them something to talk about other than the Seymour thing or our mysterious disappearance."

I felt somebody bump into me from behind, and when I turned around I found Neve standing there.

"Hey! I didn't know you were coming to this, too!" she smiled and gave me a quick hug. "I'm here with Arthur, he's in business, doing his MBA."

"This is a new one?" I asked, raising a brow. She was quickly catching up to me in her number of guys. I was impressed, she had really taken to the lifestyle like it was natural for her. It was nice to have somebody else in my life that understood the attraction, and it would be really amazing to have parties or game nights with other people like ourselves.

I wouldn't have to pretend they were just my roommates, or worry about somebody coming over just to get the inside dirt on how we lived our lives. I could relax among people like myself.

"This is a new one," she whispered scandalously. "The other two are at home, and Arthur knows the deal and is really interested in it."

"You're a beautiful, sexy women," I said close to her ear. "Who wouldn't be interested? He'll be lucky if you choose him."

"Thank you," she said and continued. "Without you, I never would have had the guts to do this you know. I didn't even know I was allowed to."

The song I'd wanted to dance to ended, and another banger started. I wasn't going to miss this one so I finished with, "You can live whatever life you want. That's the amazing thing about relationships."

"You're so right," she said and I hugged her again before heading onto the dance floor with my Kings.

It was just as daunting as I thought it would be, and I probably could have used another couple of glasses of wine to really bolster my confidence. I didn't have time to go back and gulp them down before swimming into the ocean of judgmental business majors.

I caught Neve's eye from the sidelines as she sat with her new guy, Arthur. She nodded at me, giving me a look of approval. I appreciated her support, I needed anything I could get.

And then I caught Blackstone's glinting, obsessive eyes watching my every move. The smirk on his face as he stared at me completely erasing the idea of him being a nice guy.

I hated it when my instincts proved wrong, the first time I met him I didn't think anything bad about him. In fact, he'd come off as being pretty chill for one of the richest students at Fincross.

But now, as he locked his hooded eyes on me and I felt the weight of his gaze, I could see that had been an act. He wanted me, I knew that now. I wanted to take me away from my Kings, to possess me and own me. He was the type who didn't want anybody to have me if he couldn't.

He was used to leading the way. He had everybody around him jumping and running at every little command he barked and he couldn't figure out why I didn't respond the same way. Maybe that's why he had done something with Seymour. Maybe it had been a deliberate attempt to disrupt my life from the moment I met him.

I shuddered and broke away from him at last, turned away and fell into Kingston's arms.

"Are you okay, Evie?" he asked. His voice was gruff with his concern. "You look concerned."

"And this is time for you to look sexy and seductive," Ryker said, standing protectively closer to me. "Who's bothering you?"

"Who do I need to punch in the face?" Archer asked in my ear. "Somebody's fucking with you."

"How do you guys know?" I asked, slowly moving against Kingston's body as the music began to pick me up again. I couldn't ignore it once the beat caught me, my body wanted to move the same way it wanted my Kings. I loved dancing, even with weirdo wannabe alpha losers trying to stare me down into submission.

I wasn't the submitting kind, but he didn't know that.

My Kings did, and they knew when I was unsettled by somebody, they could read everything about me. From the twitch I got around my mouth when I was unhappy, to the stiffness in my neck when I was uncomfortable.

I loved how in tune they were with my needs, even when I was being intimidated by an asshole who may or may not have been the reason I wound up in jail.

"Whoever it is, they aren't worth your time or worry, princess," Valen said, pulling me toward him. Kingston loosened his arms and let me go, Valen enveloped me and kissed my neck.

I wanted to tell him about my suspicions, but how could I? The music was too loud and the crowd was bumping against us, too close and full of curiosity about our unusual relationship. We were destined to cause a scene when we were out and open about it, that wasn't the part that bothered me. What bothered me were the leering men and their gross stares. They didn't even try to hide the way they licked their lips or gave us sidelong glances of lust.

So I ignored them all, it was the only way I could deal with them. I sunk into the sensation of being with my Kings and the freedom of not hiding it in public. I let them run their hands down my body, I threw my head back and closed my eyes, and fell into the bliss of our energy.

The song changed to something with a throbbing beat

and we danced even closer together. I could feel them all pressing against me, encircling me and protecting me from all the prying, spying eyes with their tall, muscled bodies. I was safe inside of our whirling, twisting cyclone of dancing and touching, loving and expressing our love.

Not hiding it was incredibly uplifting. Normally in a situation like this, we would work so hard to keep our love from everybody, but now we didn't care. We wanted them to know.

Once the music stopped, we barely managed to sit down long enough to eat the dinner they served. This was followed by long, boring speeches about the future of business and the importance of connections and I thought I was going to lose my mind.

I wanted to get home and have my Kings, and I wanted to follow up with the private investigator. They were warring ideas in my head, each battling for space, but since I couldn't get in touch with the private investigator until the morning I knew which one would win.

The one that was ever present and completely at my fingertips.

My Kings.

"Can we ditch this boring stuff and get home?" I asked Archer as I leaned against him.

He glanced at me, then up to the person who was speaking, and back to me.

"We're supposed to be making connections, princess," he said, then looked down to his thigh where my hand was sliding up towards his cock. "Then again, who needs connections when you have Ivan Popolov on your side?"

He groaned as my fingers danced across the ridge of his thick cock and his eyes glazed over the moment I began to stroke him through the fabric of his pants.

"I think our little whore queen needs to get home,"

Kingston said from my other side. He was well aware of what I was doing, and luckily there were only the five of us at our table or else it would have been extremely impolite. It was one thing to dance slowly with each of them on the dance-floor, but it was quite another to be practically jerking them off under the table with other people present.

I liked to think I wouldn't be that gauche, but evidence would point to the contrary. When it came to my Kings, I wasn't exactly a shrinking violet.

"Take me home," I whispered to Kingston, then looked over at Ryker and Valen. "This is boring to me, I feel weird as fuck with Blackstone eye fucking me from across the room, and I need to go back to where I feel normal and safe."

"And where's that, princess?" Ryker asked in a low tone, his eyes hooded with desire.

"In the middle of the bed with all of you surrounding me. It's the only place I feel like I can be truly free and it's the only place where I feel like I can relax. I know I'm loved and nothing bad will happen to me when I'm in your arms."

"Fuck it, we don't need this shit," Archer said, standing quickly and sliding his chair back with an audible screech. His hard on was fully visibly down his left thigh and it was right at eye level with me. I couldn't help but stare, as if I was in a trance, and I wouldn't break free until he helped me stand.

I took his hand and the five of us left, weaving between the tables and the crowd of business majors. Neve gave me a knowing look as we left, and I winked before turning away.

Several people said goodbye to them, and the speaker fell silent until our disruption was finished and we left the room.

"Looks like somebody forgot to turn the kettle off," the speaker joked and titters of nervous laughter filled the room behind us.

"God, I'm so glad to get out of there," I groaned when I heard the joke.

We practically ran to our SUV and I fell into deep, sensual kisses on the way home. It felt like no time passed at all, we were so enthralled with each other.

That was the most amazing thing of all, every time we wound up together, every time I touched them, it felt like the first time all over again.

I was carried into the house when we got back, and I didn't even know who was holding me as the took turns kissing and loving me. I was enveloped in it all and deeply lost to the sensations when we stepped through our front door.

"I was wondering when you'd get home," my mom's voice greeted us, and just like that, my safe, happy bubble was popped and I was dragged back into reality. "I have to talk to you about Reg and Nat and what we're gonna do here."

"About what?" I asked, meeting her gaze as shock coursed through me. She'd aged years in the few months since I'd seen her, and she looked like she'd gone through several plastic surgery, filler, and Botox appointments in that time.

"Your sister is coming to live with you while Reg and I move to Mexico. I can't stand the little bitch, and Reg reminded me how much he loves me so I'm leaving her with you."

"The fuck you are," I said, but the moment I said it, I knew it would happen just like that.

Mom's eyes were telling me she knew what Reg was capable of at long last, she was no longer blaming me for what had happened.

"Wait, what did he do?" I asked, and braced myself for the response.

CHAPTER 15

"He didn't do anything yet," she said, pulling out a pack of cigarettes and fumbling to open them. "But I see the look in his eyes and I think about what you said."

"So you'd rather send her away to live with me than give up on that abusive asshole?" I asked, sneering at her. I could feel hands on my back, comforting me.

"I'd rather give her the best life she can have," mom replied, putting the cigarette on the edge of her perfectly painted red, puffy lips. She dug in her Chanel purse for a lighter. "You're gonna provide it, because I can't."

"There's no smoking in here," Kingston said, his voice a coiled serpent of tension. He wasn't pleased with my mom's appearance, not because of Nat but mostly because she was upsetting me. He hated that, they all did.

"What are you gonna do about it, neighbor kid?" she scoffed and pulled the lighter from her bag. It was gold and encrusted with diamonds with her initials in blood red rubies. I wondered how much of Nat's money it had cost and realized she was right. Nat would be better off without her as the only parental figure. It would have to be me.

"We're going to make sure you respect Everly's house," Ryker said, stepping towards my mom. "Please give me the lighter or take it outside."

He held out his hand, polite but insistent and full of the message she needed to hear. She wasn't in charge in this house, she couldn't walk all over me, and her bullshit wasn't welcome.

"I'll smoke at the hotel," she said. "I'll tell Nat to bring her shit in, she can stay the night and move in I guess."

"Wait, what?" I stammered. "She's here with you? Why did you make her stay outside?"

"I figured you'd turn us down if you knew," mom replied. She was more sneaky animal at that point than my own caring mother. I wondered if she'd ever been a mother to me or if I'd just imagined her as more loving so I could cope with my life somehow.

"I'll come out to get her," I said, leaving back through the front door to the driveway. Mom had parked on the street a short ways down from the house so we wouldn't notice her there.

I saw Nat hunched over in the passenger seat scrolling on her phone, completely checked out of reality as the glow from her screen lit her face up. She was beautiful, that was one tragedy, she would have a harder life because of it. She had been exposed to enough bad stuff that she understood the power of her beauty at too young of an age, and that was the difficult part of it all. She had a sharpness about her aura that made her dangerous, depending on which side the blade was facing.

She would need help learning to direct it towards the right kind of people, those who deserved it. Perhaps she even carried the same darkness that I had inside and I could help her redirect it outward, against horrible bastards who needed to be hurt.

"Hey brat," I said as I opened the back seat of mom's little car. I took Nat's bags and slung them over my shoulders. Archer reached for them one at a time and took them from me as my Kings showed up to help.

God, I loved them.

"Hey," Nat replied, miserable as could be. "I'm sorry about this."

I supposed that was one good thing about having a psycho for a mother who would abandon you at the drop of a hat. It was humbling and made you realized the ground you were standing on could dissolve beneath your feet at any time. Nat's normal arrogance was gone, replaced with fear and a subdued hope for acceptance.

"Don't you dare apologize, I was just telling the guys the only thing that would make this life better would be my sister living with me again," I smiled and shut the back door. Nat opened the passenger side and slid out, stood in front of me, and wiped the tears from her eyes with the back of her hand.

"Sure," she said, but a smile played around her lips. "I'm sure that's the exact thing this horny sex house needed. An annoying little sister showing up with her fractured life and fucked up family."

"Your fucked up family is my fucked up family, remember, you dork," I snorted. "Everything you're going through is normal, because our lives aren't."

"Thanks," she said again and looked behind her at our mother. "And thanks for nothing."

Nat flipped our mother the double bird, extending her middle fingers on both hands and clicking her long nails together.

Mom smiled, but her face fell as we walked away. I couldn't read what she was thinking, but I hoped it hurt.

When I turned back to look at her, she was inhaling her

cigarette and a cloud of smoke already hovered above her head. She didn't wait long, it seemed.

"So, let's get you settled," I said brightly. "You didn't bring much, did you?" I asked, eyeballing the two oversized backpacks my Kings carried ahead of us.

"Mom wouldn't let me take anything she bought," Nat said. "She wanted to keep it all, the clothes and make up and everything."

"The joke's on her, because she looks like shit," I laughed. "She's aged a decade cine I saw you guys last."

"It's all the stuff she had done to her face," Nat said, moving her hand across her own nose and lips. "She wants to be a real housewife of Oakville or some BS like that."

"Ridiculous," I said, emphasizing each syllable so hard that Nat laughed when I finished. I liked making my little sister laugh, and I would like making her life better. I should have never left her alone with our mom.

And despite our evening plans to get down and dirty had been ruined, I was still excited to have Nat the brat back under my wing.

* * *

"Do you think she'll ever be happy again?" I asked after a week of Nat living with us.

"She will, I promise," Kingston said, as we watched Nat spar with Archer and Valen. She was back on the path learning how to defend herself even though she tended to make fun of me for being too paranoid.

She hadn't started school in person again, private or public, but had chosen to go fully online for the rest of the year. I worried she would become too antisocial, but then I remembered how she'd started partying back in Oakville and was grateful she was kind of a recluse.

"Nice form," a familiar voice said and I whirled around to find Amara standing in the doorway of our small training building. We'd installed it in our back yard so we could still work out while at college.

"Amara!" I exclaimed, and much to her surprise, I grabbed her in a huge hug and squeezed as tightly as I could. "I can't believe you're back!"

I stepped away and looked her up and down and nodded with excitement. She looked good, she'd healed and she looked healthy. It hadn't even been that long since I'd last seen her, but she'd done well with herself.

"I couldn't leave you alone, now, could I?" she said with her usual deadpan tone, but she was smiling. "I mean, who would be around to test you?"

She made a quick move towards me and I blocked her, tried to punch back and wound up on the floor on my back before I could see her hand and leg move.

"God dammit," I laughed as she stood over me. "Why did I always fall for that one? You fake an opening, I take it, and you sweep your leg."

"Every time," she grinned and helped me to my feet. "Your sister could use some more training, you know. Will you have her long?"

"Forever, it seems," I said and pressed my lips together to fight back the wave of emotions that rolled through me. It still hurt at times, realizing that our mother had chosen Reg over either one of us.

And yet I was still grateful that Nat was with me and not in Reg's gross predatory hands.

"Your mother letting her man dictate her family again?" Amara asked and watched Nat spar with Ryker.

"He's still around and he's still calling the shots," I said. "But he's dangerous, too. Imagine that, knowing what your husband did to your daughter and what he's capable of doing to your next one and yet you turn your back on them and stay by his side."

"It's a fucking shame," Amara spat, her bitter emotions unable to be contained. "I can't fathom that sort of thinking."

"I don't know what to do with Nat, she seems okay but I worry she'll get into trouble if I can't give her the time and attention she needs."

Amara nodded, understanding where I was coming from. She turned to me and got into a fighting stance once more and said, "We'll talk about it later. For now, I want to knock you down a couple more times just to remind myself that I can."

She meant it with all the good humor in the world, but her words teased a red anger up from the pit of my stomach and I attacked.

We carried on like that, back and forth, for half n hour or so and she even let me win a couple of rounds.

When we finished, we walked to where Nat was still working out. This time she was alone and punching a hanging bag with all her might. I could sense the coiled rage inside of her, all the unspoken things that needed out, and it worried me.

I didn't have that kind of dedicated work or time to put into her if I was going to stay in school. And I'd fought so hard to finish the semester and move into my third year that it felt silly for me to drop out now.

Amara was assessing her, I could tell by the way she kept careful watch of Nat's movements and by the little nods she made every time Nat made a good strike with her fists or feet.

"I could help," she said at last, and as soon as she spoke my little sister stopped in the middle of her workout, turned around and squealed.

"Amara!" she exclaimed and threw her arms around our friend. "You're here! I was wondering what happened to you, I haven't seen you in Oakville for so long now."

"I've been travelling," Amara said, stiff at the attention but clearly pleased with the affection. "I'm sorry I didn't write you a letter or send a postcard."

"Or text!" Nat said and stepped back. "You could have texted me, I missed our weekly runs."

"You two were running?" I asked. I didn't know Amara and Nat had been that close after I left.

"I liked to check in with her, yes," Amara said. "I don't know if I'm more like and aunt or a big sister, but I feel close to the two of you. I know I don't say it enough."

"Holy shit, if you're expressing emotions, you must be dying," I whispered, but laughed to let her know I wasn't serious. I was touched by her words, but I had just as hard of a time letting people know how I truly felt. I loved Amara like family, but didn't know how to tell her.

"I think more like an aunt, maybe," Nat said and looked at me. "I already have one big sister and she's kind of annoying, so I think I'd prefer having a cool aunt instead."

"Sounds good to me," Amara chuckled and walked towards the hanging bag. "So are we gonna keep at this, or what?"

Nat nodded and began hitting the bag again while Amara gave her instruction on her posture and her strikes.

I walked away from them with my heart full, knowing they were there for each other and they could help their much needed healing by working together.

I watched my Kings for a little while, then did some cardio on the treadmill before dinner.

By the time we got back into the house, we were one big family again, just like before.

It felt natural to be together, and it felt good to have everybody I loved under my roof. Now all we needed was for Ivan and Penny to show up, and my life would feel complete.

134

CHAPTER 16

"So you see, Blackstone and his family arranged the entire thing," my private investigator said on the phone a couple days later. "They paid her off, set her up with the new place, and tried to take you down. It wasn't personal, though, remember that."

"It's hard to think about it like that when they got me thrown in jail and on the run from the law," I said, but agreed to lay the matter to rest.

We hung up after I got details on how to send his final payment, and I still didn't feel good about the incident after we were done.

He'd found Seymour and had convinced her to come back to Fincross. She'd been paid an enormous sum of money to take a few months off and had jumped at the chance. Lucky for me, she was alive and willing to return. Unlucky for me, it seemed as though the Blackstone family had it out for me and Ivan.

They might be working on the same side with Ilya, but having cut him down at the knees meant the Blackstones were weakened even if they didn't know it yet.

My mind swung between being angry over them targeting us for seemingly no reason, and feeling free because they didn't scare me as much as I thought they would.

I had become numb to the danger at that point. I was unable to let fear course through me when I'd already beaten back anybody who'd come for me. I was ready for a peaceful life, a boring life, even if it meant burying my head in the sand.

"What happened?" Amara asked when she walked into the living room and found me on the couch after the phone call. "You look depressed."

"It's nothing, really," I replied, not wanting to upset her or worry her over my continued drama.

"Did they find the professor?" she asked, flopping on the other end of the sofa.

"She's alive," I said and exhaled, realizing how much tension I'd been carrying in my body once it was released with each breath out. "I don't even know what they were trying to achieve, maybe just to fuck with me. Maybe Avery was right, and they needed me arrested to get my attention."

"Who knows what these assholes do or why they do it," Amara asked, leaning her head back and closing her eyes. "I think the only thing you can do now is focus on what you want from your life and go get it."

"I have most of it already," I said. "I don't know what else I want or need, I guess it doesn't matter as long as I've got my guys and my family."

"What about me?" she smiled and opened one eye halfway to look at me. The sun was shining in through the tall windows off the garden and she was glowing as if underwater. She was pretty when she wasn't tense and killing people. I still wished she'd end up with Ivan and become my step-mom, but beloved cool aunt would have to do.

"You're family, dork," I said and kicked her foot with mine. She laughed again and closed her eyes once more.

We talked for a while, going over the possibilities of my life and hers, what we could do with Ivan's businesses and what she planned on doing after she left our place.

At last I heard Nat tumbling down the stairs from the guest side and it made me sentimental for the days we lived crammed in the tiny house in Oakville. As much as Nat thought she was grown up and basically and adult, hearing her coming down the stairs like that made it clear she had one foot in childhood even at her age.

I hope I could help her cling to her innocence for as long as possible, to not find out just how dark the world could be until she was mentally prepared to handle it…and physically able to kick some ass.

"What are you guys talking about?" she asked, sitting in the big, soft chair near me.

"Life and the future," I said. "I can't believe I still have a couple years here at Fincross, what are you going to do for that time? Do you want to enroll in school here?"

"Fuck now," she said and shook her head. "I can't handle the thought of changing schools. If I stay here with you, I'll stick it out online."

"What if you came back to Oakville with me?" Amara asked, sitting up and opening her eyes.

Nat and I were both stunned, neither one of us had ever considered this as an option.

"You mean to live with you?" Nat asked, her eyes brightening at the thought.

"Yes, if that's okay with Everly," Amara replied. She looked at me and raised her eyebrows.

"I mean, if you want to," I stammered. "It would help out a lot, and then Nat could keep training and stay around her old friends. As long as she's not around the bad influences, it would be great."

"I don't let bad influences stick around for too long," Amara warned. "In fact, you'd have to agree to my rules if you wanted to live back in Oakville. I'd expect your grades to stay high and for you to take your life seriously. No drinking or smoking or partying with friends. And definitely no loser men hanging around. Or boys. No men or boys."

"My boyfriend broke up with me, so there's nobody else," Nat replied evenly. "And I agree to the rest, I just want to make it through high school and get to college where I can figure out my life."

I didn't want to tell her that college didn't exactly help with figuring things out, I was just as confused as ever. How could I? She was so happy to be going back to Oakville.

"And I guess best of all, you won't have to live with us," I laughed. "I know how much you hate it when you see me kiss any of them."

"I mean, it's kind of weird," Nat said, screwing up her face. "Even you have to see that."

"I do," I replied. "And I understand which is why I keep our PDAs to a minimum when you're here."

"Well, when I'm gone you can do whatever you want, wherever you want," she said, frowning as she continued. "Not that I even want to think about that. Gross."

"Thanks," I chuckled. "Okay, it looks like it will work. You can take her back to Oakville and get her set up. I think our mother is pretty much gone at this point, so if you need anything signed then let me know. I have legal guardianship of her at the moment."

"Only for another couple of years," Nat protested. "Then I can do what I want."

"That's also not quite how that works," I laughed. "But we'll cross that particular bridge when we get to it."

We talked some more about the arrangement and Amara agreed to fly her out the next day.

I loved having Nat around, she was my little sister after all. But having her around the house really disrupted the energy of our lives. And worrying about her interrupted my schooling. All around, this was the best option for all.

* * *

They stayed a few more days just to get some shopping done and to get a few things wrapped up. When it came time to drive them to the airport to take our private jet back home, I was gripped with a strange feeling.

I knew everything was changing and it felt strange to me. The next time I saw Nat, she would be even more grown up. This visit might have been the last time she ran down the stairs or laughed loudly like a little kid. She was growing up fast that I couldn't keep up.

I suddenly wanted to beg her to stay with me, and to stay little. I knew it wasn't going to happen, and going with Amara was ultimately the best thing for her, but it still hurt to hug her goodbye.

"You look like you're going to cry," she said when we broke off our embrace.

"I feel like I'm losing my bratty little sister," I said. "You're already taller than me, the next time I see you you're going to be as tall as a model."

"I wish," she said wistfully. "Maybe Ivan could help me with that. And before you say anything, i know, I know, he's not my father but I love the way he treats you. I wish I had that."

"I know, but you do. In a way, you do. He loves you because you're my sister, and we're all family even if we're not related by blood. And my Kings, you know they see you as their sister. They'd do anything for you, just like me."

I held her face in my hands and kissed her forehead before letting her go. She stepped back, flipped her long, blonde hair so much like our mother's, and turned to walk towards the plane.

Amara gave me a mock salute, smiled at me and sent me a look of reassurance that quelled the nerves inside.

She would take care of Nat the brat, and I could finish my studies here, hopefully uninterrupted at this point.

"Are you gonna be okay?" Ryker asked on the drive home. "This has gotta be hard."

"It's weird," I said. "I haven't thought about her that much because of everything we've been through. I also thought she was safe with our mom, but finding out that I dropped the ball with that and she was having trouble? That bothered me more than anything else lately."

"You didn't drop the ball, princess," Archer said, taking my hand in his. "You're so busy making sure everybody else is taken care of that when you think about yourself, it feels selfish."

"Your parents made you look after Nat from day one, so no wonder you think she's your responsibility, Evie," Kingston said.

Valen rubbed my knee to comfort me, he didn't need to speak, I knew that he agreed with the others.

When we got home, there was enough time to make dinner and get some studying done. We'd all caught up as much as we could, but I still had a couple of things I needed to finish.

Once I was done, I stood and stretched and looked around the room to where my Kings were reading or on their laptops.

"I think it's time for bed," I said deliberately, and none of them moved.

"I said, I'm going to bed," I said louder, looking around. I cleared my throat and said, "It's time for—"

Kingston reached out from the couch behind me and grabbed me by the hips. He pulled me back onto his lap and I wiggled around, laughing and breathless at his quick moves.

"Did you think I didn't hear you," he growled and nuzzled my neck. "Of course I did, I had to close my laptop, Evie, love."

His hand slid down the front of my yoga pants and he cupped my pussy through the fabric. He gave a quick squeeze and nibbled my ear.

His hot breath heated my skin and sent shivers down my spine. I closed my eyes and felt his hands on my body and listened to the ragged sounds of his breathing. His scent engulfed me and the love I felt for him was all around me.

I felt another hand join his, and then another, and when I woke my eyes I found the rest of my Kings around me on the couch, their eyes burning with lust and desire.

"I definitely think it's time for bed," I said and stretched again before wiggling to sit up on Kingston's lap. "I've finally reached the age where I want to fall asleep after we have sex, and I don't want to move."

"I think we've all reached that point, princess," Ryker agreed with a chuckle.

We stood up together, but before I put my feet on the floor, I was swept up in Archer's arms.

"We'll make sure you're taken care of, love," he said and the intensity in his eyes took me off guard. He loved me deeply, they all did. They loved me with the fierceness of protective guardians, like loyal bonded mates, we'd be together until the very end.

I still didn't know what I'd done to deserve such devotion,

but I felt it right down into my bones. At the cellular level. Their love and care had become part of me from the physical to the emotional and spiritual. I was nothing without my Kings, and they were nothing with me.

I tucked my head against Archer's chest as we went upstairs for a much needed release of lust before falling into a slumber in each other's arms.

I didn't know where our lives would take us, and I didn't know if we had decades or days left together. I could hope for years and years, until we were all old and wrinkled, but life wasn't predictable. That was one lesson I'd learned the hard way in the time I'd been alive.

I didn't even know what had happened to some of the worst people in my life, like Thackeray's wife, the others in the Organization, Ilya, Maksim or even Avery. I didn't want to know what was going to happen with my mom or with Reg.

But when I was with my Kings and we were safe at home, none of it mattered. I would spend a lifetime forgetting about the bad people I'd known and focus on the ones I loved.

I would see Penny when she came to visit, and I would see Nat and Amara and Ivan when I returned to Oakville for Christmas.

Archer put me down at the top of the stairs and I walked into my room with my Kings by my side. Before I had any more time to ponder our existence or the outcomes of those who had wronged me, Valen dropped to his knees in front of me and slid my pants down over my hips, completely distracting me from anything else.

They stripped me naked in no time, and as I was placed gently onto the bed, I could feel their mouths all over my body. I took a deep breath and sighed, allowing myself to sink back into the bliss.

Nothing else mattered, only love and what we had here in the moment.

The world outside disappeared and I let myself go as they kissed me to the heights of ecstacy that I could only find with my Kings.

<h1 style="text-align:center">EPILOGUE</h1>

EPILOGUE

I STRETCHED AND FELT THE WARMTH OF THE SUN ON MY SKIN as a light breeze crossed over my body. I was tanning next to our pool at the Fincross house and I was almost falling asleep.

The sound of a distant lawn mower was hypnotic and the chirps of birds in nearby trees was the lazy soundtrack to my perfect life.

I was at the end of my third year of school, which meant I had one more to go for my Bachelor's degree.

Everything was working out for me, and even though there was the constant fear that I'd lose it all somehow in the back of my head, I finally learned to appreciate my life.

Even the craziness with Seymour from last year had faded into distant memories. She'd come back to class and found me one day to apologize. I didn't hold anything against her, she had been paid an enormous amount of money to take a vacation, there was no way she could have known what would happen to me after she left.

Ilya had recently died of a heart attack, at least that was the official story. When I asked Ivan about it, he had twitched his mouth into a smirk and tried to look sad about it but had failed.

I suspected he got his revenge, but since we were trying to relate to each other on positive, happy levels now, we hadn't brought it up again. Maksim, predictably, was blowing through his father's estate at such a rapid pace I didn't think he'd be rich for more than another year or two.

Penny and Mark had gotten engaged recently and she'd finished all her final exams which is why she was here with me now. She was snoozing on the comfortable lounge chaise next to me and I could add her light snoring to the sound-track of my perfect life.

My Kings were off playing a friendly game of football with Mark and some other guys from college so we were taking advantage of the opportunity to have our down time.

Ivan and Amara were bringing Nat tomorrow, and we had plans to travel as a group to do two weeks in Europe, just for fun this time. I wanted to be a tourist during this trip, not a captive, and I wanted to discover different cultures with the people I loved.

I couldn't wait to do a private tour of the Louvre with Nat, or visit an opera house in Vienna with Penny.

Or get naked and busy with my Kings in every city, to reclaim all of Europe for our pleasure and strip away any lingering feelings of fear.

It would be good for us all.

I began to doze off myself when I heard them return. It wasn't so much that my Kings were noisy, they were, but it was a shift in energy in the house when they were there.

I could feel them coming before I heard them, like a tsunami of love hormones and desire for me, it washed over me and left me breathless.

They clattered out onto the pool deck, talking and laughing all at once and dragging the lazy energy off me.

I laughed and let them kiss me, one by one. They pulled chairs over to sit near me while Mark shared the chaise with Penny.

And they destroyed the silence of the afternoon with spirited descriptions of their game and arguments over who really had won.

I smiled and listened, exclaimed where appropriate, and overall, loved hearing it.

As much as I loved the quiet peace of my life when they were gone, I much preferred the busy whirlwind when they returned.

My life was better with them in it, and I wouldn't change it for anything in the world.

I smiled and nodded at their excitement, and fell in love all over again with each one of them. I would be their queen, their dirty queen wearing my dirty crown as long as they were my Kings.

My loves, my life.

THE END OF SERIES

If you'd like one more peak into their lives, check out Covington Christmas!

ABOUT THE AUTHOR

Sign up for my newsletter to keep in touch. Find out about beta or ARC opportunities, get sneak peeks at new books, and have access to giveaways!

http://eepurl.com/hBcvpr

Scan the QR Code to find my newsletter!

facebook.com/Author-Amelia-Winters-110161967967643
instagram.com/author.amelia.winters